THE THREE
COFFIN CAPER

THE THREE
COFFIN CAPER

DAVID BRUCE

authorHOUSE®

AuthorHouse™
1663 Liberty Drive
Bloomington, IN 47403
www.authorhouse.com
Phone: 1-800-839-8640

Published by AuthorHouse   11/13/2012

ISBN: 978-1-4772-9078-1 (sc)
ISBN: 978-1-4772-9077-4 (e)

Three coffins lie on the ground. The mourners gathered
round. But, would the cause be found?

CHAPTER ONE

It was seven o'clock in the evening on Tuesday May 8, 1945. This was a special day because this was Victory in Europe Day. People were dancing in the streets. Women were kissing strangers, soldiers and sailors in Times Square. World War II was finally over. The boys would be coming home. Parents were ecstatic. With a little luck, their boys would make it home in one piece. The word of the day was relief. People left work early. Tears of joy were common. Hitler and his minions would not be taking up residence in America after all. The world held new promise.

Chester Brantley parked his forty-one Packard in the lot adjoining the Santa Fe Building in which he maintained his office. The Spanish architecture of the building was well suited for the location in the downtown area of Orange, California. The building resembled some of the Spanish missions that Father Junipero Serra founded up and down the length of California. Brantley was a private eye. He would celebrate in his second floor office with the bottle he kept in the bottom right hand drawer of his desk. He would have a drink with the boys at Mack's Bar later. The night air felt cool and fresh as he approached the front of the building. Just as Brantley drew near the front entrance the doors exploded, and the concussion knocked him on his back. The dust and smoke swirled over his prone body in a dense cloud. Suddenly in his mind he was back in the South Pacific. Brantley's ears rang as the lights grew dim and went out. He didn't hear the ambulance come to get him. He didn't see the crowd of people that gathered.

The nurse at the hospital checked over his muscular body looking for injuries. She noted six foot tall, approximately two hundred pounds. His chest looked like a size forty eight, and his biceps were about twelve inches around. A fine physical specimen to go with his square jaw, rugged good looks, and short cropped black hair. She checked his hazel eyes for signs of a concussion, but found none. The nurse got his age, of thirty two, from his private detective's license. She noticed the eagle tattooed on the back of his left hand. Must be an ex-serviceman, she thought.

Two hours later Chester saw a blurred vision of loveliness standing over him. The figure of the young woman was dressed in white. "Are you an Angel?" he mumbled.

"Only my mother thinks so," said the nurse smiling. "Take it easy you have had a hard knock."

"Am I missing anything important?"

"No, you are all in one piece with a terrific bump on your head."

Chester touched the knot gingerly and whistled. "Any idea what happened?"

"You were too close to a bomb when it went off."

"What? I thought the war was over."

"It is, but someone is trying to blow up the city piece by piece. There have been two bombings here in Orange and five in Los Angeles."

"My God! The work of fifth columnists?"

The nurse replied, "No one seems to know. The radio is full of the news, but nothing concrete about the cause of all this chaos. You are lucky this happened to you here instead of in Los Angeles. They say the emergency rooms over there are loaded with victims."

"Was I the only one hurt at my office?"

"The shine man who worked in the barber shop was killed leaving the building."

"Oh, no, not Sam. What did he ever do to anybody?"

"Don't worry about it now, Mr. Brantley. You've had quite a shock." The nurse slipped a needle into the private eye's arm and said, "Just relax".

Chester Brantley lay back as fatigue claimed him once more and he drifted down a long black chute into senselessness. His dreams starred an unassuming shine man named Sam. Images of a slender black man in white pants, white shirt, and white smock filled his head. Comfortable emotions accompanied the images. Sam had been shining Brantley's shoes for years, even before the war. Joe the barber had been cutting the detective's hair for just as long. Brantley had returned to Orange in 1942 when discharged from the army. The bullet he still carried adjacent to his spinal cord had earned him an early discharge. He kept the Purple Heart he received in the bottom left hand drawer of his desk. He might meet someone who really deserves it someday.

CHAPTER TWO

The California sun streaming through his hospital window awakened Brantley the following morning. When he opened his eyes he saw the same nurse leaning over him taking his pulse. "Are you still here?"

The nurse replied, "No, but I'm back on duty. We are pulling twelve hour shifts since this mess started."

"Have there been more bombings?"

"None in Orange, but two more in Los Angeles."

"What's your name?"

"Miss Williams."

"No first name?"

"First name is only for friends."

"Tough cookie. I'm not your enemy."

The nurse smiled, "Maybe we will meet under less professional circumstances someday."

"I would like that. When do I get out of here?"

"The doctor signed your release an hour ago. There are two detectives waiting outside, to get your statement."

"Show them in, Beautiful, by all means. Let's not hold up the long arm of the law."

David Bruce

Two men in suits entered the room and approached the bed. Both men were tall and heavy muscled. "Chester Brantley?"

"Yeah, that's me."

"How are you feeling?"

"Well, I have felt better, but it looks like I will live."

"I'm Detective Sergeant Logan, homicide, and this is my partner, Detective Reynolds. Can you tell us what happened last night?"

"Not much to tell really. I was walking up to the door of my office building and all hell broke loose. I woke up here later."

"Have you got any reason to believe the bomb was meant for you?"

"No, I don't think so. They tell me we are having quite a rash of bombings."

"That's true, but we have to check out all the angles. Do you know Sam Lewis, the colored shine man in the lobby barbershop?"

"Sure do, nice guy. Good family man."

"No reason you can think of to believe they were after him?"

Brantley replied, "None that I know of."

"Okay, here's my card. If you think of anything else, please give me a call. This case is a high priority."

"You know I'm a private investigator, I guess."

"Yes, you're not working on a dangerous case are you?"

"No, just divorces and stuff like that right now. These bombings sound like fifth columnists to me."

"Whoever is behind these bombings must be stopped."

6

"I agree with you. If I turn up anything, I will give you a call."

After the policemen left, Brantley got dressed in his blue surge suit and pearl grey hat and took a cab to his office to pick up his car. The office doors were being replaced by the maintenance man. Brantley saw the chalk outline of a man on the floor near where the heavy glass doors had been. Sam had expired there. Joe the barber was in the shop sweeping up glass. The large front window of his shop was shattered, too.

"Brantley stepped to the door and said, "I'm sorry about Sam, Joe."

Joe jumped at the sound, "Wow, I guess I am jumpy today. Yeah, it's a bad break. Sam was a good man. I'm going to miss him. Ches, come in the back room for a taste. The two friends walked around the glass on the floor and sat at the barber's desk in the back room. Joe poured them two fingers each from the bottle of Jack Daniels. They sat in silence till they finished their drinks and cigarettes.

"What do you make of it, Ches?"

"So many bombings in one night between here and Los Angeles, it must be related to the war."

"It's a crying shame, Chester. We go through this struggle for four years and then the minute you think everything is going to be okay . . . Well, you know what I mean."

"I know exactly what you mean. I'm mad as hell. If I had my way, I would barbecue the bastards that did this myself."

Joe said, "If you get a chance give them hell for me." Tears rolled down the cheeks of the usually tough minded barber.

Brantley stood up saying, "I'll do that for you, Joe. You take it easy. Sam would want it that way."

The barber poured himself another drink as Brantley walked out of the room and took the elevator to his office. The picture of Harry Truman hanging over the desk in his one room office gave Brantley a little comfort.

Chester liked President Truman. To the detective Harry was an unassuming haberdasher. He had the courage to put a sign on his desk saying, "The buck stops here." If other politicians were half the man Harry was, the country would be in a lot better shape.

The bottle in Chester's desk would help even more. The no frills office oozed manhood. Two wooden chairs stood in front of the desk for clients, a large heavy wooden desk complete with Underwood typewriter, accented with stacks of papers, and an ink pad complete with fountain pen and a half filled bottle of ink. The bare wooden floor reflected stability. Chester Brantley Private Investigator was stenciled on the green corrugated glass of the door. The two bare windows overlooking the street had just the right amount of dust to depict a busy man's lair. Brantley sat at his desk puffing on a Lucky Strike and typed out a report to Mrs. Ronald Crandall informing her that her husband was indeed spending time with his secretary. When he finished the typing, he put the report in an envelope and poured himself a stiff one. His thoughts ran back across the events of the last few days. What kind of world is this? Demure little wives broken hearted over philandering husbands, innocent shine men getting bumped off for no reason, buildings blowing up all the way to Los Angeles. Brantley went home for a much needed sleep.

CHAPTER THREE

The next morning found Chester Brantley sitting at his breakfast table catching up on current events with the local Thursday newspaper. This week has been two weeks long already, he thought. The paper was full of the war and the bombings. The writers were seeing fifth columnists behind every door. In Los Angeles the train station was hit, the bus station, the Hollywood branch of a local bank, and a cab company. Then Brantley read the stories of the Orange explosions. The newspaper carried the story of Brantley's office building and a local diner. Diner? Why such a small place? Humph? Brantley dressed for work and drove the Packard to the office.

Over the phone Brantley said, "Mrs. Crandall, I have your report ready. Would you like to come down to discuss it, or would you rather I just mailed it to you? I wouldn't want your husband to open it by mistake." Mrs. Crandall made an appointment for twelve. Brantley made some calls until noon and then reviewed his report with the lady. She cried and made him feel like a heel. After her cry she paid him and left. Thoroughly disgusted with life, he decided to have lunch at Mack's Bar. He put on his hat carefully to avoid the knot on his head and walked the block to Mack's place.

"Hey, Chester. How are you today?

"Need a Jack Daniels neat. Hell, make it a double."

"How are you doing, Buddy? I read about you getting hurt."

"Mack, you know they can't hurt me hitting me on the head."

"Okay, tough guy," Mack said laughing.

Brantley sat at the bar nursing his drink. "How about a ham on rye, Mack?"

"Coming right up."

When Mack returned he said, "Here you go, Chester. I have been wanting to ask you what you think of all this craziness."

"I'm still trying to take it all in. The bus station and the train station, the bank, and the cab company make sense for fifth columnists, but why blow the doors off an office building and blow up a dinner in Orange? Something smells fishy. Transportation, banking, and a greasy spoon. What a combination. I need to check out who's renting in my building."

Mack shook his head and walked away laughing. "It's too deep for me, Buddy. Let me know when you get it figured out."

Brantley finished his sandwich and his drink and returned to his office. The lump on his head was beginning to hurt again. If it were Friday afternoon I would go home, he thought. With resignation he began working on a skip trace he was doing.

Being a gumshoe is ninety-seven percent boredom, he told himself.

BLAM! A blast shook the building.

Brantley was startled, "Damn, what was that?" The detective jumped up and sprinted out of the office and down to the street leaving his hat behind and the door open. He hurried past the downtown circle. People were talking loudly and milling about, horns were honking, and the sidewalks were full. Everyone seemed to be headed in the direction of the Orange train station. Smoke and dust seemed to be rising from that area. The station was only two blocks away. Chester followed the crowd, aware of a growing sense of dread. As he walked past the Orange post office he saw a young soldier walking in his direction. The corporal's uniform was freshly pressed but his hat was missing and the young man's face was as white as a sailor's cap. Brantley looked down at the sidewalk and saw that a stream of blood was following the soldier. The sea of onlookers parted for the corporal. He walked up to the detective and said. "They got Tommy." The corporal swayed. Brantley grabbed the soldier's arm and eased him into a reclining position. The stricken man's gaze seemed far away. "I thought we won the war."

Brantley waved his hand in front of the soldier's unseeing eyes. "You and Tommy did win the war. You're back in California. You just had an accident."

The corporal said, "It's night already, I can't see a thing." The young man coughed once and went limp.

"Mister . . ." Brantley turned to see a young lady kneeling beside him. "That was a nice thing you did."

"What?

"You helped that boy die at peace."

"That was the least I could do for him."

With unbelieving eyes, Brantley surveyed the remains of the train station. The open air station had collapsed with the explosion. Debris and a number of bodies littered the concrete platform. Several men desperately tried to flag down an approaching train. Women screamed in anticipation of the impending catastrophe. The tracks were destroyed in front of the station. Chester pulled his .45 automatic from his shoulder holster and fired it twice in the air. The engineer of the train, seeing and hearing such a commotion, slammed on the brakes. The train ground to a halt just short of the wrecked tracks. People stood and stared with shocked expressions. Clearly America was in trouble. Had the war in Europe come home to them?

Brantley looked at the bodies lying near the wrecked railroad platform. One of them would be Tommy. Sirens blared and police labored to clear the area of onlookers. Chester walked back to his office. He grabbed his hat, locked the door, and walked down to Mack's bar. The radio was playing "Rum & Coca Cola" by the Andrews Sisters. He sat at the bar and watched the confusion as people in a half shocked condition wandered in and spoke nervously with each other. Chester was no stranger to this sort of scene. He had seen enough of this sort of thing in the South Pacific. His hand began to tremble, so he shook off the dark memories. He watched the short slender figure of Mack as he hustled drinks for the customers. Mack O'Donnell was a wiry little Irishman with a smile for everyone. Rita, the curvaceous night bartender, wouldn't be on till later. Mack turned on the radio and the excited announcer gave skimpy details concerning the train station bombing. Some congressman made a statement concerning the German American Bund being responsible. He said something about the FBI being busy tracking down Nazi sympathizers even as he spoke. Chester thought, anti German sentiment will be running high, and a lot of innocent people could get hurt. Chester said aloud to no one in particular, "Next thing you know we will have German camps like those for the Japanese."

"Ready for another drink, Chester?"

"Rita, I didn't see you come in."

"Just as safe here as at home. Things are getting scary."

"The usual, Sweetheart. You'll be all right, you're too tough to let a little trouble get you down." Chester knew that Rita had been a promising reporter in Los Angeles with a master's degree until she stood up to the city editor and got herself fired. He felt that she was wasting herself in Mack's bar, but she liked the people and he valued their friendship. Her ample curves made anything she wanted to do okay with him.

Rita brought Chester his drink and looked deep into his eyes. "Chester, we're closing early tonight because of all the chaos and I don't want to go home alone. I know we don't do this too often, but I would love to have your company." Her throaty voice made her even more irresistible.

"Of course, Sweetheart. I will wait for you." Being with Rita always gave Chester a burning sensation in his chest. Thinking about her made his blood pressure just a little bit higher. Rita had style and grace. Her hair was long, curly and brunette. She had a beautiful olive complexion, her face had a perpetual look of youth, and her heart was as sweet as nectar.

Rita was five foot four inches tall, with ninety eight pounds of curves that gave promise to men's dreams.

Rita smiled a sweet smile and went about her duties. Chester nursed a couple of drinks as he waited and listened to the radio. President Truman gave an address to the nation and promised a resolution to the problem would be forth coming. The news reported that the governor of California had stopped short of declaring marshal law by ordering the National Guard to protect the train stations, airports, bus stations, and certain banks. Chester saw Joe the barber coming up behind him in the bar room mirror.

"Chester, I'm glad I found you."

"What's wrong, Joe? You look worried."

"Maybe I'm crazy, but . . . ."

"Take it easy, Joe, have a drink. It can't be that bad." Chester ordered a drink for his friend and watched him take the first swallow."

"Okay, that's better. I went to see Sam's wife, Georgia. She's got me all upset."

"Calm down, Joe. What did she say?"

"Chester, she says that Sam got a call from his son in the Army. She said that Sam acted different after he received the phone call."

"Different in what way?"

"She said he started carrying a gun."

Chester looked shocked. "Sam? That's hard to believe."

"Georgia says, he had trouble sleeping and seemed worried."

Chester looked to the right as he thought about what he had heard. "Did you notice anything different about him, Joe?"

"No . . . Yes . . . Oh, I don't know. He was always a quiet kind of guy. But, that isn't all. She received a visit from an army officer today. Sam's boy has been killed in some sort of accident."

"For God's sake," said Chester.

"There's more, Chester. I went back to the barber shop. Sam had a 38 Smith and Wesson in the drawer in his shine stand."

Chester Brantley stared Joe in the face wondering what to say.

"Rita, give us another round." The detective pondered the information.

"Okay, let's just remain calm. Soldiers do get killed in accidents and fathers do worry. The gun and what happened to Sam worry me though. All this is odd if you link it all together. Let me sleep on it, Joe."

The Jack Benny radio program came on Mack's radio. The announcer read a commercial for Lucky Strikes. The two men's thoughts were far from comic. They scarcely heard a word of the show. The program was signing off when Chester and Joe got up to leave. Jack Benny said his usual, "Goodnight folks." Rita turned out the lights and accompanied Chester out the door. They both told Joe good night and walked to Chester's car. They sat silent all the way to Rita's apartment. Chester remarked, "Did you notice all those Army uniforms on Chapman Street?"

"Maybe it's the National Guard?"

"Could be, I guess."

Rita made them coffee and they cuddled on the couch. Rita looked long into Chester's eyes. He ran his fingers through her hair and kissed her hard on the lips. She kissed him back. It had been too long since they had been together. After several such kisses Rita excused herself and went to the bedroom. In a few minutes she returned wearing a night gown. Chester could see the outline of those beautiful curves of hers through the gown. She kissed him soft and warm and pressed her body against his. Her softness seemed to melt into his form. Chester kissed her long and slow. His heart beat faster and he noticed her eyes were dilated in passion. It had been too long for her, as well.

Chester whispered, "Let's go, Sweetheart."

The two lovers got up and walked into the bedroom. Rita turned out the soft light of the lamp by the bed.

An hour later, two men attached packages of explosives to two pillars of the Queensway Bridge in Los Angeles. They placed the packages carefully to inflict maximum damage. They worked in the dark with experienced hands. Carefully they placed detonators with timers. They set the explosions to go off in half an hour. Then they drove away and were miles distant when the explosions collapsed one end of the bridge. Two cars drove off the end of the bridge before the damage was discovered. The following day hundreds of commuters would need to be rerouted to work.

CHAPTER FOUR

The next morning over coffee and eggs Chester perused the newspaper. He saw the report of the bridge bombing. Then, his eyes stopped cold when he saw the headline of a small article on page four, "Shine Man's Wife Commits Suicide." The short paragraph stated that Georgia Lewis had committed suicide evidently as a result of depression over the death of her husband, Sam Lewis, in the Tuesday night bombing of the Santa Fe Building. Her body was found in the park during the night.

"Damn it. What in God's name is going on?" Chester asked through gritted teeth.

"What's wrong?" said Rita.

"Sam, the shine man, died in the bombing the other night and now his wife has committed suicide. Holy shit, everyday it's something new."

"Take it easy, Chester. There's nothing you can do."

"The hell there isn't. I'm dealing myself a hand. I'm tired of watching people die. This is America. You don't just come over here and start destroying our hometown and bumping off our citizens. Where is your phone book?"

The detective looked up an address. Then he showered and dressed. He drove to 2514 Seventh Street. He parked around the corner and removed his hat and coat before taking a clipboard from his trunk. He paused to roll up his sleeves. He walked up to the door of the bungalow and knocked. He called out, "Oh, Mrs. Lewis. It's the repairman. I'm here to do the estimate for you."

Chester checked the mail in the box and put it back. He looked under the mat for a key to no avail. Finally he pulled a ring of skeleton keys from his pocket and deftly opened the door. Even though the outside of the house needed painting the inside was neat as a pin. The cops hadn't tossed the place. The detective went through some papers on the kitchen table. There was the letter from the War Department. Private Reggie Lewis died in an accident in New York City on his way home. He fell off a subway platform and was hit by the train. Chester borrowed the letter and placed it in his pocket. Georgia's purse was open on the table. Chester wrote down the phone number from the little tag on the phone. He found a bundle of letters, tied with a ribbon, in Georgia's vanity. They were from Private Reggie Lewis. He borrowed them, too. After giving the place a thorough going over, Chester locked the door and left. He returned to his car and drove to the medical examiner's office.

Chester put on his hat and coat and walked into the office. He showed his badge to the secretary and asked to see the M.E. The girl didn't seem overly impressed, but after talking on the intercom, she sent him in. The sign on the door said, "Dr. Herbert Sloan Medical Examiner." As Chester walked in he heard, "What's up, Chester? Working on a case?"

"You could say that." Chester took a seat across from the taciturn man in the doctor's smock.

"I'd offer you a drink, Chester, but it's too early."

Chester smiled, "The way things are going, I wonder if it is ever too early."

"Things are a hell of a mess, aren't they? What brings you to see me?"

"A friend of mine bought it in all this. And I got laid out for awhile, too."

"So I heard, Chester. Feeling okay now?"

"Yeah, I just have a sore head. Sam Lewis and his wife haven't been so lucky."

"Oh, that's it. You know something's wrong about both those deaths."

"That is the kind of info I need. What did you find, Herb?"

"The lady was found shot to death in the park, an apparent suicide."

Chester responded, "That's what the paper said."

"Yeah, but something is wrong. She was shot with a .45 automatic. Women don't use that kind of hardware. In all my years I have never seen a woman use a big bore gun like that. She was a little petite woman, too."

"Really? The paper didn't mention that. I think you have something there. Did she have a purse with her?"

The M.E. thought for a minute. "I don't remember one being turned in with the body. I'll check." The doctor got up and left the room. Two minutes later he came back into the room.

"How did you know, Chester? She didn't have one with her. She had one shoe missing, too."

Chester said, "Keep it under your hat, but her purse is sitting on the table in her kitchen right now. Herb, women don't go to the park in the dead of night barefoot to commit suicide with a .45."

The M.E. sat with his mouth open. "Chester, I think you are on to something this time. I would sure like to hear how it comes out."

"Don't worry, Doc, I'll let you know what I find out. Wait a minute; you said there is something wrong with both cases. Is there something funny about Sam's death, too?"

"Well, I have my suspicions. He was struck from the front by flying glass, and metal, and landed on his left side. The peculiar thing is he had a contusion behind his right ear that looks exactly like someone sapped him. The cause of death was loss of blood, but he could have been unconscious when it happened."

"Okay, Doc. Thanks for the info, and I will get back to you."

"Please do."

Chester left the office and returned to the Santa Fe Building. He called the landlord's secretary and asked if there were any new renters in the building. He asked her if she had any idea why the building had been targeted, but she had no clue. Chester sat at his desk and called the phone company. After inventing a story, he was able to get a list of long distance calls coming into Sam's house for the last month. A collect call had been placed by a Reggie Lewis to that number on May first at eight o'clock in the evening from a New York City hotel.

Chester lit a cigarette and exhaled slowly. He felt his head where the bump had been. It was still sore. He turned the facts as he knew them first one way and then another. He walked down to the corner drug store and ordered a sandwich and bought a paper. The paper said the explosions had been claimed by a group called The German Workers League. Chester sat at one of the tables placed on the walk in front of the drug store. He could see the circle from his chair. The traffic circle, or plaza, was right in the heart of the downtown district. Onlookers would never know it, but there were tunnels under the circle connecting the office buildings. During prohibition there were speakeasies, gambling dens, and even ladies of the night plying their wares in those tunnels. Chester thought, the way things are going people will be using them to escape bombs. He got up and walked to the police station.

The detective climbed the stairs of the municipal building to the second floor. He stopped at room 212. Homicide was stenciled on the door. He asked the first detective he saw if Detective Logan was in.

"He's down the hall having coffee with his partner." Chester walked down the hall to the coffee room the cop pointed out.

Logan saw him enter the room and waved him over. "What brings you here, Brantley?"

"Thought maybe we should compare notes."

"Sounds good to me. What have you got?"

"I don't like to spill my guts, but there is something funny here. Sam the shine man's wife committed suicide the other night."

Logan replied, "I heard about that. That's a bad break."

"She was only wearing one shoe and not carrying a purse. Seems kind of peculiar to me."

"Hysterical women do strange things, Brantley."

"Did you know their son died in an accident just a few days ago on his way home from the war?"

Logan sat in silence for a few seconds, "That might help explain the suicide."

Chester lit a cigarette and blew the smoke at the ceiling.

"Just the same, it smells fishy to me. Have you got a line on any of the bombings?"

"Not really, our experts say dynamite was used, but we have no leads on the source of the dynamite. It's all academic for us anyway."

"What do you mean, Logan?"

"We expected the FBI to take the investigation of the bombings away from us, but Military Intelligence is doing their best to take it away from them. So, we are officially off the case."

Chester replied, "This thing gets murkier and murkier all the time. I don't like it."

Sergeant Logan scratched his head, "Just between the two of us, I don't like it either. Officially I can't do anything, but if you want to pursue this thing you can call on me unofficially."

"Thanks, Logan. I'll let you know. Take care of yourself." Chester nodded to Reynolds and walked out of the coffee room.

Brantley walked out of the building and up the street deep in thought. If things are as they seem, why are all the bombings in Orange and Los Angeles only? Why would fifth columnists strike only here instead of Washington or New York? Chester stopped in at the newspaper building. He went to the newsroom.

"Is Charley in?" he asked.

The young kid replied, "He is in his office."

Charley Tate was a short fat man. He had been the editor of the local paper for years. He was a no nonsense kind of guy, who could smell a story miles away. Chester stopped at the open door of the editor's office.

"Can a guy get a drink around here?"

Charley Tate looked up from his desk and straightened his glasses. "Sure thing, Chester. Come in." The bald headed newsman took two coffee cups from a drawer and poured two fingers of scotch in each cup.

"Here smoke one of my stogies, too." Chester and Charley removed the cellophane from the smokes and sniffed the essence of good tobacco.

Chester said, "Charley, you are living the high life, now. These are fine cigars."

Charley smiled, "I'm a widower now, Chester. I can afford to splurge a little."

"I didn't know, Charley. Blanche was a good woman."

Charley smiled, "She was a pain in the ass, but any woman that could put up with me for thirty years would be."

Chester tried not to smile, "You have a point."

Charley refilled their glasses, and offered a toast, "To pain in the ass wives. God bless em." Charley leaned back in his chair. "How are things going for you, Chester? Is your back doing okay?"

"Doing good Charley, but I don't like the way things are going lately. These bombings don't make sense."

Charley squinted his eyes as he looked intently at Chester. "What bothers you about them?"

"Well, why is southern California the only target and why Orange? Why not hit the East? Why is an unassuming shine man, his wife, and son all dead within a few days of each other?"

"His son? I didn't know about that. When did that happen?"

"The boy was killed in an accident in New York, a couple of days before Sam, on his way home from the war. Another thing that stinks is Sam's wife said Sam had been upset since talking to the boy on the phone, and was carrying a gun."

Charley said, "This is beginning to smell like a story."

Chester said, "Charley, something is wrong here, but I would appreciate it if you would sit on the story for awhile. I could use your help though."

"You can count on me, Chester. Did you hear about the explosion at Huntington Beach this morning?"

"No, was anyone hurt?"

"Yes, several people were injured. It happened at the pier. Someone blew up one end of it."

Chester responded, "Charley, it gets crazier all the time."

"Just be careful, Chester. This whole thing could blow up in your face."

"Don't I know it? Charley, I would like for you to check out the kid's accident. He supposedly fell in front of a subway train in New York. He called his dad from this phone number. The date and time are here. It would be good to check out any other long distance calls he might have made. In addition, I would like to know the name of his outfit, the conditions of his discharge, if possible the where a bouts of his army friends, and anything else we can dig up."

Charley blew smoke toward the ceiling and replied, "I will get right on it. Do you have the same office and home number?"

"Yeah, here is another one of my cards."

"Chester, I know some of the victims of these bombings are soldiers. I'll check out that angle, too. I'll get back to you as soon as I find out anything."

Chester finished his drink, bid Charley farewell, and left the building. He threw the butt of the cigar in the street as he walked along. He thought, what am I forgetting? I know something is eating on me, but what? Chester stopped off at Mack's and ordered a beer. Mack brought the beer and left Chester to his thoughts. The bar was surprisingly busy for three in the afternoon. A number of soldiers sat at the bar, and others played pool at the tables. After two beers Chester waved to Mack and started back to his office.

Joe was cutting hair. Chester sat in a waiting chair near the door. The barber smiled at him and continued talking to the guy in the chair. They were talking about the war, the occupation, politicians, and who knows what else. Chester thought, the good thing about barbers is they know all the answers. It must be nice.

In a few minutes, the barber chair was empty and Chester took the seat. "Trim it up good, Joe. You know how I like it."

Joe draped Chester with a chair cloth and put a Sanex strip around his neck. Then he wrapped the chair cloth snugly over the strip and attached the clip to hold it in place.

"How are things going, Ches? I haven't seen you going and coming much lately."

Chester replied, "Oh, I've been trying to check out a few things."

"Ches, I know you like to keep your own counsel, but I am interested to know if you are following up on this. I wouldn't ask, but I have a reason."

"Joe, we have been friends for a long time. I don't mind telling you what I am doing. I am looking into the bombing and what happened to Sam."

"Have you turned up anything?"

"Mostly just questions so far."

Joe pulled a stool over to the barber chair and sat down. He looked Chester in the eye. "Chester, Sam made me the executor of his will. He had a little money set aside and his house is paid for. The insurance policies will bury Sam, Georgia, and Reggie, and they didn't have any living relatives. So, there will be money left in the estate that will come to me. I would like to hire you to pursue this matter. How much do you charge? I don't know about these things."

"Joe, I don't want your money. I'm doing this because it affects friends of mine, and because it may be a threat to the country."

"Don't get excited, Chester. I'm not trying to steal your thunder, but you shouldn't have to bear the brunt of this alone. Your time is worth money, and this way you can afford to work on it full time for awhile."

Chester stared off in space for a few seconds. "I hate to take your money."

Joe cleared his throat, "It isn't really my money, Chester. It's Sam's an I feel that it is the right thing to do. I cared about that guy. We have worked together, side by side, for years. It doesn't matter to me what color he was. He was my friend." Tears ran down Joe's cheeks. He got up and got a towel to wipe his eyes.

Chester watched his friend from the barber chair. He rubbed his cheek and said, "Okay, Joe, I usually get twenty bucks a day plus expenses. I will take the case for half that."

Joe replied, "You will take the twenty a day, damn it. I can handle twenty days. If that doesn't do it, we'll renegotiate."

Chester smiled and said, "Okay, you old bastard, now can I get my haircut?"

Joe smiled and wiped his eyes, and went back to cutting hair. "I will give you a check for two hundred to start."

Chester sat quietly while Joe worked. He thought, what am I forgetting? I know there is something I am missing.

"Joe, do you know what regiment Reggie was in?"

Joe stopped the clippers and said, "I think Sam said it was the Fighting Forty-ninth."

"Do you have any army officers for customers?"

"Sure I do, some of the officers stationed at the Santa Anita Barracks." The government had set up a Japanese internment camp on the parking lot at the Santa Anita horse racing track. The Japanese were only held there a few months and then moved inland. Afterwards the camp was used as a barracks.

"Okay, Joe, now we are getting somewhere. See if you can verify Reggie's regiment and check on his record. Also, try to get an officer's eye view of these damn bombings. Can you do that for me? I will talk to the guy myself if you would rather."

"No problem, Chester. I am glad to help. I'll let you know as soon as I find out something. The funeral for Sam and his family is tomorrow at the little colored cemetery. I chose Saturday morning because Sam's friends cannot afford to miss work."

"That was a good idea, Joe. I will be there."

Chester noticed Joe looked pleased to be involved in some way in the investigation. He thought about what a gentle person Joe was to be such a big guy. He stood five foot ten inches tall, two hundred and ten pounds. The barber's two middle fingers on his right hand were missing from an oil well accident that occurred when he was a young man. However, Joe used the scissors with his right hand as well as anyone. Chester shared a drink with his friend before returning to his office.

Chester hung his hat on the rack and sat down at the desk. He poured himself two fingers from the office bottle and lit up a Lucky. He leaned back in his chair and blew a smoke ring at the ceiling. He switched on his desk radio. Perry Como was singing "Until the End of Time." What a voice that guy has, he thought. Chester thought about Sam, Georgia, and Reggie. He thought about the soldier he watched die near the train station. He thought about the news reports of German bunds, fifth columnists, and German workers' unions. Then he remembered the letters from Georgia's vanity. Chester took out the little bundle of letters.

This is what I have been forgetting he told himself. They were tied with a pink ribbon. Some of the envelopes were tear stained. One by one he read each letter, feeling like a peeping

Tom. They were the letters of a lonely soldier far away from home. He didn't name his regiment, just his APO address. He wrote about missing his parents and his girl friend, Wanda. He complained that colored soldiers were treated differently than the others. He felt that his main contribution to the war had been peeling potatoes and helping to load trucks. He said some of the officers were particularly callous. The letters were wordy, and reading them was time consuming. Chester smoked half a pack of Lucky cigarettes and drank several stiff ones before he finished the last letter. He noticed it was dated one week before Reggie's death. Reggie explained that he was being cashiered out, but didn't give a reason. He mentioned that he had worked on a secret assignment.

"Humph", Chester said to nobody in particular. He sat up and stretched. He was getting stiff and looking at his windows he noticed it was dark outside. Chester stood up and leaned back popping his back. That felt better. Feeling a little tipsy, he decided to get a bite to eat at Mack's Bar. The detective picked up his hat and coat, and locked the door behind him. The hallway was dim and the floor made hollow thumps as he walked past the darkened doors of the neighboring offices. The elevator operator was gone, so he took the stairs. As he neared the front door, he paused at the spot where Sam had expired. The chalk marks were gone, but still vivid in the detective's mind. Chester used his key to let himself out, before turning toward Mack's place. The air was nippy but refreshing as he walked the block. The street lights gave forth a yellow glow. Groups of soldiers in well pressed uniforms strolled the walkways, laughing and chiding each other. Some had escorts and looked pleased. Jeeps with pairs of military police drove by. Music filtered out of crowded bars into the street.

Chester waved to Mack as he entered the bar and took his favorite stool. The juke box was playing Les Brown's new record "Sentimental Journey" featuring the pear shaped tones of Doris Day's voice. Half the people in the bar were soldiers and their dates. Rita was behind the bar serving beer with both hands. She smiled a 'hello' to Chester. Without being asked, she brought him a Jack Daniels.

"Hi, Stranger, long time no see."

"Yeah, not since this morning."

"I thought you would spend the day with me."

"I'm sorry, Gorgeous, I have been working on a case."

Rita smiled, "Since when has a case excluded me from your life?"

"You've got me there, Beautiful. No case could be more important than you."

"Ches, you are such a sweet liar." She grinned at him.

Chester smiled and said, "What's going on, the place is lousy with soldiers. I haven't seen this many uniforms since I got out of the service."

"You've got me, Sweetheart. The town is full of uniforms and stripes. The tips are good though."

A sergeant called out, "Service, can't a guy get any service here?"

Rita smiled at Chester, "Oops back to work." She wiggled just slightly as she walked away for the detective's benefit.

Chester had just started his second drink when a fight broke out in the pool room. A corporal was trying to extricate his date from the embrace of a drunken soldier.

"Get your damn hands off her, you bastard." The private was trying his best to kiss the pretty redhead. She didn't seem to care one way or the other, but the corporal wasn't having it. He let loose a beautiful haymaker and the private dropped like a duffle bag off the back of a truck. The would be lover lay on the floor with a silly grin on his face, staring at the back of his eyelids.

Suddenly, a ham fisted MP swung the corporol around and planted his night stick on the surprised soldier's forehead. His date screamed as her hero fell to the floor unconscious.

"What did you do that for, you big ape?"

The military policeman did resemble an ape. He had huge bicepts and forearms with legs to match. His teeth had a definite yellow tinge to them, and there was a gap between his two front teeth. The brute yelled back at her with a scowl, "He was drunk and disorderly."

Wincing from the smell of his breathe the redhead screamed at him, "He isn't drunk, you bastard."

The girl drew back her hand to slap her opponent, and the gorilla raised his stick once again. Chester stepped between the two of them.

"Watch it, big guy. You aren't really planning on using that horse cock on a lady are you?"

The six-foot-three soldier lowered the stick. "I suppose not," he said. "But, this guy is under arrest."

The private eye answered, "For what? Before you answer, think about the fact you are talking to a veteran of the South Pacific. So, be sure you mean what you say."

The MP scowled and stepped back. "He was drunk and fighting."

Chester lit a cigarette and said, "He didn't look drunk to me. He was protecting the lady's honor. The one on the floor is drunk. You can have him, if you like."

The MP gritted his teeth and picked up the private and carried him out to the street. Chester and the redhead picked the corporal up and set him in a booth. Rita brought a wet towel and some smelling salts. It was not long before the soldier woke up complaining of a headache. Rita brought a bar towel full of ice for the knot on his head. Chester told the redhead, "I think he will be alright, now. Keep an eye on him."

"Thanks, mister, you saved Jack a lot of trouble."

"Don't mention it. I was glad to do it."

Rita brought Chester another drink. "You stuck your neck out, didn't you, Ches?"

"I don't like bullies. Everything is going nuts around here lately. I am getting fed up with it. I am about ready to take a poke at somebody myself."

"I know what you mean. Did you hear the evening news?"

"No, why?"

"A navy ship was sunk at San Diego."

"Sunk!"

"Well, they said there was some kind of explosion and it sunk."

"They aren't saying it was fired on, are they?"

"I don't think so. They didn't mention ships or submarines or anything. Honey, don't get so excited."

For a moment Chester's mind was reeling. Was this war? Was it fifth columnists? Too many questions. Too few answers. Chester sighed and took a long drink.

"This mess gets worse every day."

"Want to stay at my house tonight?"

"I had better just go home, Rita. I have a triple funeral to go to tomorrow."

"Are you sure you will be alright, Ches?"

"I'll be fine. Maybe things will look better in the light of day."

Rita gave him a kiss saying, "I'll take a rain check on that night at my house."

Chester smiled and said, "That is a date."

The detective picked up his hat and walked out into the breezy May evening. He drove home and took a shower before hitting the sheets. The bed felt good to his weary body.

While Chester slept, the bombers were at work once again in Los Angeles. A lone figure appeared by the window the of the post office on Los Angeles Boulevard near China Town. He placed the bomb next to the window adjacent to a large bank of mail boxes. The timer was set for eight in the morning.

The following morning business people were hurrying to pick up the mail on the way to work. Most businesses were open six days a week. Tomorrow would bring a well deserved rest. The clock struck eight, and the post office window shattered with a great explosion. Twenty people were killed instantly, and numbers more were injured. People ran screaming from the building. Sirens blared, chaos reigned. Would there be no end to these atrocities?

CHAPTER FIVE

In Orange, it was a beautiful day. The sun was shining and the breeze chilled the cheeks of the mourners at the cemetery. Three caskets rested side by side. The mourners were mostly colored people. The tears flowed as the minister made his final comments. Chester stood with Sam's friends and Joe stood beside the caskets. Flowers surrounded the graves. Sam and his family had been well liked. Tears rolled down the cheeks of the minister. Sam had been active in the church. Numerous young people, friends of Reggie, were in attendance. The feeling of loss hung heavy in the air. Sam's friends shook hands with Joe and some hugged him. Joe's eyes were swollen from tears and loss of sleep. He had sat up with the bodies all night.

As the mourners began to disperse, Chester stepped to Joe's side. "How are you doing, Joe?"

Joe's voice broke as he said, "It's pretty tough."

Chester shook Joe's hand and said, "I know."

The two friends stepped aside as the funeral directors lowered the caskets. They walked slowly to their cars and lit up cigarettes as the cemetery boys covered the graves and placed the flowers over the sod.

Joe said, "I guess the hardest part is over."

Chester replied, "I want to ask you a question, Joe."

"Shoot."

Chester said, "I hate to bring it up today, but did you know Reggie had a girl friend named Wanda?"

"Yeah, I met Wanda. Her last name is Jennings. She is a nice kid."

"Was she here today?"

"No, Reggie's best friend, Charles, said that she went missing."

"Missing? When did this happen?"

"She didn't come home from work two days ago."

"Do you know where she works?"

"She works for the Sunshine Laundry on Main Street."

"Where are you going from here, Joe?"

"Some of Sam's friends are having a big lunch at his church. I thought I would go over there for awhile. Would you like to come along?"

"No, I want to follow up on a couple of leads. Try to get some rest, Joe."

"I will, Chester, thanks for coming. Let me know if I can help."

Chester drove to the Sunshine Laundry on Main Street. He talked to the manger who introduced him to Wanda's supervisor.

"Tom, this is Chester Brantley. He is looking into the disappearance of Wanda Jennings. See if you can help him."

"Yes, sir, I will."

The manager returned to his office leaving the two men in the noisy laundry. "Would you like to go to the coffee room, Mr. Brantley? It's difficult to hear anything out here."

"That would be good."

The supervisor lead the way to the coffee room and the door swung shut behind them. It was much cooler and quieter.

"Would you like a cup of coffee, sir?"

Chester said, "Thank you."

The two men prepared their respective cups and sat at a table across from each other. Chester offered a cigarette to the supervisor. They both lit up and exhaled the smoke.

"Now, Mr. Brantley, what can I do for you?"

"I understand that Miss Jennings hasn't been to work for a couple of days. Is that right?"

"Yes, she worked late the night before last. Normally I would not think anything of her absence, but she has not called in. Her mother called the next morning looking for her. The girls say her boyfriend was killed in an accident. Elizabeth said she saw her talking to a man in the parking lot after work and we haven't seen her since."

"Did the girl get a good look at the man?"

"I don't know. Would you like to talk to her?"

"Yes, I wouldn't keep her long. If you don't mind."

The supervisor smiled, "The boss said to do what I can to help. I'll be right back."

Chester looked around the room as he waited. There was a Bunn coffee setup like in a café, some tables and chairs, but nothing fancy.

In a few minutes, the supervisor returned with an attractive young black girl.

"Mr. Brantley, this is Elizabeth. I explained to her that you are looking into Wanda's disappearance."

"Good morning, Elizabeth. How are you today?"

"Okay, I guess. Are you some kind of cop? I don't care for cops."

"No, ma'am, I am a private investigator. I am not trying to arrest anyone. I'm only trying to help find your friend. Nothing you tell me will cause you or Wanda any grief. I promise you. Is that a fair deal?"

"I guess it's okay. I would like to help Wanda. She's my friend. I hope she is okay."

Chester said, "I understand you saw her with a man after work the other night. Is that right?"

"Yes sir, I was walking through the parking lot on my way home and I saw her talking with a young man."

"Could you hear what they were saying?"

"No, sir, they were just standing there looking at each other and talking." "Can you describe the man?"

"He looked like he was maybe twenty something. He was wearing a bright colored sport shirt and khaki pants."

"Could you tell how tall he was and his hair color?"

"He was a white man with dark hair and about five foot eight, I think."

"What about the length of his hair and the look of his body, Elizabeth. Was he skinny or fat?"

"No sir, he was kind of physical looking. You know what I mean?"

Chester replied, "You mean he was athletic looking?"

"Yeah, that's it, and his hair was short. He looked kind of like a ball player or something."

"Now, for the big question, could you identify him?"

"They were standing in a dark area. I don't think I could identify him, sir."

"Elizabeth, is there anything else you can tell me?"

"No, sir, I don't think so."

"Did you see Wanda leave with the man?"

"No, sir, they were just standing there talking kind of intent like."

"Did anyone else see them together, Elizabeth?"

"Not that I know of, sir."

"Okay, I guess that is about it. Do you always work on Saturday around here?"

"Yes, sir, we always work on Saturdays, except for holidays."

"Well, I am glad I was able to talk to you. Thanks again for your help. Here is one of my cards. If you think of anything else give me a call. Okay?"

"Sure thang. Thank you, sir. I wish you luck. Not many white men would try to help colored people."

"Good luck to you, Elizabeth."

After Elizabeth left the room the supervisor said, "If you leave me your card, I will call you when Wanda shows up."

After giving the card to the supervisor, Chester excused himself. He drove back to his office building and sat down to think. Another person missing or dead. What does it all mean? Everyone surrounding Reggie is dead or missing. Reggie said he was working on something secret. A colored young man who complains of KP and loading trucks who says he worked on something secret all of the sudden.

Chester called the medical examiner. "Hi, Doc, this is Chester Brantley. Does everybody work on Saturdays?"

"No rest for the wicked, Chester. What can I do for you today?"

"You don't have a Wanda Jennings down there, do you?"

"No, not that I know of. I do have an unidentified colored girl that came in last night."

Chester set up in his seat, "Uh oh. What is her age, can you tell?"

"She looks to be about twenty or so, Chester. Could that be the girl?"

"I think so, Doc. Someone should be able to identify her. If I am right, her name is Wanda Jennings and she works for the Sunshine Laundry on Main Street. The supervisor can ID her. Have the cops check it out. Oh, Doc, what was the cause of death?"

"I won't know for sure until the autopsy, but she has a knife womb in her side."

"Doc, if you will, call me back when you know for sure. Okay?"

"Sure thing, thanks for the tip, Chester. Do you have any idea what is going on?"

"Not yet, Doc, I will let you know when I find out something concrete."

"Okay, thanks again."

Chester hung up the phone and leaned back with a Lucky. The barber shop would be closed till Monday. The M.E. would probably not call till Monday either. Rita might be working.

Chester grabbed his hat and walked the block to Mack's Bar. Rita smiled at him from behind the bar and waved him over.

"How are you doing, Sweetheart?"

"How about a double Jack, Beautiful? I'm doing okay. How are you today?"

Rita grinned and said, "Okay, I guess. At least I didn't have to attend a triple funeral."

"You have a point there. Does it show that I have been to a triple funeral?"

"Not too bad, Chess. Let me get your drink."

Rita brought a double Jack Daniels on the rocks and placed it in front of Chester.

"Oh, I nearly forgot, your corporal friend asked about you."

"The one from the fight?"

"Yeah, he has a knot on his forehead to match yours."

Chester smiled, "Mine is almost gone."

Rita said, "Here he comes now."

The corporal and his redheaded girl friend stepped up to Chester's side.

"Mr. Brantley, I want to thank you for your help last night. Rita told me your name."

"Don't mention it. What is your name."

"I'm Jack Turner. You saved me a trip to the stockade, and I appreciate it."

"That's okay, Jack. You have a sweet right cross. You really put that private's lights out."

"I do a little boxing against other guys in the army."

"No wonder you have such a good right hand."

"I'm fighting tomorrow night at a smoker. Why don't you come by the club? It's the one on Chapman Avenue just down the street."

"I might be able to make it. What time does it start?"

"It starts at seven. I'll leave two tickets at the window for you. How does that sound?"

"That sounds good, Jack."

"Okay, we will get out of your way. Have a good evening."

Jack and the redhead went back into the pool room to join a group of soldiers. Chester watched them laughing with friends.

Rita said, "Penny for your thoughts."

Chester turned back to the bar. "I was just thinking how youth is wasted on young people."

Rita laughed, "You have that right. Can I cash in that rain check for tonight."

Chester replied, "I would be honored. I was hoping you would want company tonight. In fact, is there any chance you can get off early?"

"I wouldn't be surprised. Let me ask Mack. Oh, Chester, did you hear about the post office bombing this morning?"

"It was in Los Angeles somewhere. It's getting scary, you don't know where they will strike next."

Rita went back to work and Chester watched the customers for awhile. Woody Herman's record, "Laura" was playing on the jukebox. Soldiers and civilians in equal numbers were milling around the bar. The Saturday crowd always seemed younger than the weekday crowd. Chester tried not to think about his case, and the bombings. He knew he needed a break from it. The evening air drifted in each time someone opened the front door. May evenings in southern California were usually chilly. Chester enjoyed the fresh breeze.

Rita cruised by, "It's a date, Sailor. Give me an hour."

Chester motioned for another drink and relaxed at the bar. The night was young, but Chester did not feel young tonight. The chaos of this week had frayed his nerves. He knew he was not the only one feeling the stress of the bombings and the killings. Everyone wondered if the war was really over. Would war break out anew? Something had to give and soon. Chester nursed his drink until Rita got off and then escorted her to his car.

"Are you up for dinner and cocktails, Sweetheart?"

"I'll say I am," replied Rita.

They drove up the road to a steak house. They ordered drinks and steaks and held hands across the table.

"Chester, you look tired."

"I just need to get a little rest and recuperation. It has been a tough week for all of us."

"Have you been finding out anything?"

Chester replied, "Mostly just more questions. Tonight I am all yours. How are things going for you?"

"I have just been working and trying not to worry. You know, Chester, I never expected the aftermath of the war to be like this."

"I don't think any of us did. Just hang in there, kid. This too shall come to pass. I just hope they don't have to declare marshal law. If they do, it could really get crazy."

"Chester, one of the customers was telling me the mayor held a town meeting at city hall tonight."

"I didn't hear about it. How did it go?"

"My customer said everyone was all excited, and demanding that the mayor do something."

"What did the mayor say?"

"He said, he would set up a special commission to look into the matter."

Chester remarked, "More double talk, huh? There isn't a whole lot he can do. He's no better off than the rest of us."

Chester and Rita talked and tried their best to enjoy their meal. After eating, they went to a movie and then back to Rita's place. They had a night cap on the couch before retiring to the bedroom. Their passion took their minds away from current events to a paradise where lovers meet and while away the hours in the joy of secret places and caresses.

Chapter Six

Dawn broke bright and sunny. The air was clean and brisk. Shafts of light crept through the blinds and cut through the shadows of Rita's bedroom. The spent lovers slept late oblivious to the brightness. After a long slumber, the paramours rose and started breakfast.

Chester said, "Let's go to the beach. How does that sound?"

Rita brushed her hair back from her face. "I would go anywhere with you. You know that."

"We can go to Balboa pier. Do you care if I stop and get my fishing gear? We can sit on one of the benches and relax."

"Sure, Chester, we can go right after breakfast."

The afternoon sun found them lounging on the pier watching the boats and the sun bathers. Sail boats explored the horizon. The water was an azure blue. The white caps frolicked to the beach. Children screamed with delight as the breakers washed over them. Chester watched the tip of his fishing rod anticipating a bite. Then it came and he caught a nice mackerel. The fish shimmied furiously as he took it off the hook and threw it back.

"Ches, why do you throw them back?"

"Even a fish has a right to enjoy life. Rita, I told that corporal I would watch him fight tonight. Do you want to go with me?"

"Okay, if you want to take me."

"Rita, I would take you anywhere, but it might get pretty brutal. Can you take it?"

Rita chuckled, "Don't give me that sidewise grin. I will be fine. I see some pretty brutal fights in Mack's place."

"Okay, we had better get back to town."

Chester and Rita gathered up the fishing gear and walked back down the pier to the parking lot. They drove back up to the boulevard and turned toward home. They went by both apartments to dress for the evening.

On the way, they noticed numerous police cars parked in the downtown area. The blazing lights flickered on the buildings, and policemen were milling around. Onlookers were being held back, and traffic cops were directing the flow of the cars.

"What do you think it is, Chester?"

"Who knows, it looks like more trouble."

Chester picked up the tickets at the box office and escorted Rita to their ringside seats. Jack's redhead was sitting in the next chair.

"Good evening, Mr. Brantley. Jack will be happy to see you. You are tops in his book."

Chester smiled and replied, "Jack is tops in my book, too. How are you doing tonight?"

The redhead's eyes sparkled with excitement. "I am really revved up. I hope Jack murders this guy."

"I always knew redheads were violent. I never caught your name."

The redhead gave him a coy look and said, "Maybe I didn't throw it. I'm just kidding. My name is Flo."

"Well, Flo, I hope Jack wins, without killing his opponent."

"Maybe you're right."

The program said Jack was a middle weight and would be featured in the fourth fight. The first three bouts were uneventful but filled with action. The first match was for feather weights. Those little guys punch nonstop, thought Chester. The fourth bout started at seven thirty. Jack entered the ring amongst much applause. He was evidently the favorite. While the referee went through the formalities, Chester looked around at the crowd. A good half of the crowd were soldiers. Many of them were with dates and wearing sport clothes. Their short hair, and muscular bodies betrayed their affiliation with Uncle Sam. Many of them wore bright colored shirts and khaki pants. Suddenly Chester realized they fit the description of the man last seen with Wanda. Chester turned and looked at Rita.

"What is it, Chester?"

"I'll tell you later."

Chester looked around the audience. That description could fit a lot of these service men. It seems like all this trouble revolves around service men and too much of it is centered on the Lewis family.

The bell rang and the fight began. Jack looked sharp in black shorts and black shoes. His opponent wore white shorts with a black stripe. The two fighters stepped to the center of the ring and touched gloves. Jack was obviously in good shape and carried himself well in the ring as he began sparring with his opponent. Each man gave as much as he received.

The fight was scheduled for six rounds. The first round was uneventful, mainly both fighters were feeling each other out. The second round started off with a bang as Jack pummeled his opponent with a series of lefts and rights. His foe countered with a series of jabs and left hooks. Then Jack saw his chance and pasted the other man with a left cross and a right uppercut that bowled the surprised boxer over. The fighter struggled to get up and finally made it to his feet at the count of nine.

The crowd went crazy as the fighter struggled to regain control of his legs. The referee let the fight continue and Jack moved in for the kill. He slammed two hard jabs into the jaw of the stricken man, and then unleashed that right of his once more. The weary fighter's head snapped back and he tumbled to the mat. Jack went to a neutral corner to wait for the count.

"8-9-10", counted the referee. The fallen warrior did not move. The crowd cheered as the official raised Jack's gloved hand into the air and said, "The winnah, Jack Turner."

Jack raised both gloves over his head and reveled in the glory of the moment. His girlfriend screamed with glee and jumped up and down. Chester and Rita smiled at each other. Jack turned toward their seats to see the reaction of his ringside friends, and Chester gave him the thumbs up sign.

Flo said, "Come on let's go to the dressing room. I can get you in."

Rita looked at Chester quizzically. He responded, "I'm game."

The trio struggled through the crowd to the dressing room. Jack was sitting on the massage table getting help taking off his gloves.

Flo yelled, "Hey, Baby, that was good."

Jack smiled and his face flushed a little. "I did my best."

Flo kissed him and held his free hand. "Oh, Baby. Oh, I forgot. I brought Mr. Brantley and his girl to see you."

Jack said, "Did you like the fight, Mr. Brantley?"

"Sure I did, but you can call me Chester."

"Okay, that's a deal."

Chester said, "I know you are busy, but I have a question for you."

"Anything for you, Chester."

"Where are you stationed?"

"I am billeted out at the Santa Anita barracks."

"Are there a lot of men out there?"

"Yeah, even more now."

"Why, have there been changes lately?"

"Yes, sir, some new brass came in and took over. Some general has the place all changed up."

"Changed? Changed in what way?"

"They keep us hopping all day, now. Forced marches, maneuvers, it is something constantly. Parts of the base are off limits, too. I can't complain about the passes, though. We get more now than we did before."

"Really? That is interesting. It sounds like the general wants you guys gone all the time. Here is my card, Jack. If you notice anything else unusual, will you give me a call?"

"Sure thing, Mr. Brantley. Anything you say."

Chester and Rita left the conquering hero to his glory and returned to Rita's apartment.

"Rita, did you enjoy the fight?"

"I really did. The kid is pretty good, huh?"

"Not bad at all."

Over cocktails Rita asked, "What was it you wanted to tell me at the fight?"

"It just dawned on me that Wanda Jennings, Reggie Lewis' girlfriend was seen with a young man in a brightly colored sport shirt and khaki pants the night she went missing."

"What do you mean, Chester?"

"It dawned on me during the fight that a lot of the young soldiers wear bright shirts and khaki pants. It is just a look they like."

"So, you think the Army is mixed up with these killings somehow?"

"Everything seems to keep coming back to the Army one way or the other. I don't know what it means, yet. I'm just checking things out."

"Chester, let's just think about each other tonight, shall we?"

The detective grinned at her and said, "It sounds good to me."

The two lovers spent the evening sharing love's sweet embrace. They enjoyed that special chemistry that they shared when no one else was around. Their kisses and caresses were long and tender. Rita snuggled up to Chester's warm body and forgot all her concerns. Here there was nothing to fear. There were no explosions, no police, no people running for their lives.

CHAPTER SEVEN

Monday dawned on the city of Orange bright and breezy. Chester slipped out of Rita's apartment early to let her sleep. He drove to the circle and had breakfast at the pharmacy soda fountain. Bacon, eggs, and coffee were just the ticket to start the day.

While waiting for his breakfast, Chester looked at the newspaper. The lead story was about an attempt on the mayor's life. A passing car had rained a hail of bullets at him in downtown Orange the night before.

"That was the cause of all the excitement." Chester said to no one in particular.

When he got to the office Chester checked with the answering service. He had a message from the Medical Examiner. His hunch about Wanda Jennings was right. She had been killed by a long knife blade to the heart.

Chester busied himself finishing a skip trace he had been working on. He was able to find his man. He was now living in Santa Anna. The detective wrote a report and put it in an envelope addressed to the lawyer who had hired him. The clock on the building across the street told him it was eight o'clock. Maybe he could catch the M.E. at work.

He dialed the number and leaned back in his chair. When the girl connected him to the doctor he said, "Hi, Herb. How are you this morning?"

"I am doing fine, Chester. Did you get my message?"

"Yes, I did. Do you have an approximate time of death?"

"She died at about nine o'clock that night."

"That means she was killed not long after she left work. Who identified the body?"

"The girl's father came down with the police and identified her."

"Herb, do you have an address for the girl?"

"Yes, give me a minute." In a few seconds the doctor returned to the phone. "Miss Jennings lived with her parents at 101 Mulberry in Santa Ana."

"Okay, Doc, I got it. Could the long knife that was used be a bayonet?"

"It might have been, Chester. Yes, I think a bayonet would fit the description of the murder weapon. Does that answer any questions for you?"

"It might, Doc. I'll let you know. Thanks for your help."

"You are welcome, Chester. Take care of yourself."

"I will do that. Talk to you later."

Chester hung up the phone and went down to the barber shop. Joe was drinking coffee and reading the morning paper.

"How are you doing, Joe?"

"I feel pretty good, Ches. How are things going for you?"

"Pretty good, Joe. I need to talk to you. Have you got a minute?"

"Sure thing, Chester. Let's go in my office."

The two friends sat down at Joe's desk across from each other. "Want some coffee, Chester?"

"No, thanks, Joe. I have news, but it's not good."

"What is it?"

"Wanda Jennings was murdered the other night. The night she went missing."

Joe looked stunned. "Wow, what in the hell is going on, Chester?"

"It is too early to Say, Joe. One thing for sure, there is something fishy about these killings. It may not have anything to do with the bombings, but I suspect it does. Have you had any luck contacting your brass friends at Santa Anita?"

"Not yet, Chester. I will try to make contact today. I will let you know anything I can learn."

"See if you can get any dope on the new commander out there. I hear things arc changing a lot and the troops are restless."

"Okay, Chester, I will do my best."

"All right, Joe. Don't let all this get you down. We're going to find out who is behind all this and put a stop to it. By the way, at the funeral you mentioned Reggie had a friend named Charles. Can you get me his phone number or address? I would like to talk to him."

"I think I can. Check back with me this afternoon. I will try to have it by then."

Chester returned to his office and checked the answering service again. No more calls had come in. He left his hat on the rack, locked the door, and started making the rounds of the offices in his building. By two in afternoon he had talked to most of the people in the building, however no one seemed to remember anything unusual about the day Sam died. The detective returned to his office, picked up his hat, and went to Mack's for lunch. He had a pastrami sandwich, and washed it down with an ice cold beer. Mack stayed busy while Chester was there. The detective bought a nickel bottle of Coca Cola from Mack and returned to his office. He drank half of the Coke and poured a shot of Jack Daniels in the bottle for taste. After taking a couple of sips, he dialed the answering service to discover Charley had called. Chester dialed the editor's number at the paper only to discover he was out for the afternoon. He thought, I should have called the answering service sooner. I should have talked to all the tenants a lot sooner, too. The introspective detective finished his Coke cocktail and called Joe.

"Barber shop."

"Joe, this is Chester. Did you get that info on Reggie's friend for me?"

"Yeah, hang on a minute." The barber returned in a few seconds. "Okay, got a pencil?"

"Yes, go ahead, Joe."

"His name is Charles Pink. His address is 101 Spring Street in Santa Ana, and the phone number is WIlshire5-5555. Let me know if I can do anything else. I will try to get the other information you wanted, too."

"Okay, Joe. Have a good day."

Chester dialed the number Joe had gaven him.

A nasal voice answered, "Hello."

"Yes, is Charles Pink there?"

"He might be. Who is this?"

"No one to be concerned about. I am Chester Brantley, a friend of Joe the barber."

"Oh, yes, sir, Mr. Brantley. This is Charles. What can I do for you?"

"Charles, I am looking into the disappearance of Wanda Jennings and I would like to talk to you."

"Wanda is my friend. I'll be glad to talk to you. Where do I need to meet you?"

"I could come by your place, Charles."

"That would be great, but I was on my way out. I will be back in a couple of hours. Is that too late?"

"That will be fine, Charles. I will see you then."

"Yes, Sir, I will be here."

Chester lit up a Lucky and leaned back in his chair with his feet up on the desk. With a little luck something would break soon. The pieces of the puzzle were trying to come together. Maybe Charley was able to uncover something. Joe's efforts might pay off, too. There was enough time to go to Wanda's house.

Chester cruised out to Santa Ana and parked in front of the Jennings home. There were several people on the front porch.

A young man asked, "Can I help you, sir?"

"Yes, I would like to talk to Mr. or Mrs. Jennings."

"Yes, sir, they are here in the living room."

Chester took off his hat and stepped into the house. A man and woman sat on the couch in black clothes. Chester could see a casket set up in the adjoining room. The detective stood silently with his hat in his hand.

The lady offered, "Can I help you, sir."

"Yes, ma'am, I am very sorry to bother you at a time like this. I don't want to intrude."

"Thank you for your concern, but what can I do for you?"

"Are you Mrs. Jennings?"

"Yes, and this is my husband."

"Mrs. Jennings, I am Chester Brantley. Here is my card. I am a private investigator looking into the deaths of the Lewis family and that of your daughter, Wanda."

"You are. Can I ask who hired you?"

"It would be unethical for me to say, but I can tell you that I am a friend of Joe the barber."

"Oh, the man that Sam worked for. I know he has been very good to the family in this time. In fact, we received a check from him to help with funeral expenses for Wanda. He must be a very fine white man."

"Yes, he really is, ma'am."

Tears ran down the mother's cheeks. "If you can do anything to find out who took my baby . . ." With great effort, the lady regained her composure. "I'm better now. What can I do for you?"

Chester cleared his throat, "My apologies, but I am trying to run down any letters that Reggie may have written Wanda or his friends. They may give a clue concerning this case."

"I don't know what good that could do, but I want to help. She kept some letters in her room. Let me see if I can find them. Have a seat, Mr. Brantley."

Chester sat down in a chair, feeling like a heel intruding at a time like this. Mr. Jennings looked like a boat with no oars. His face portrayed emotions that shifted first one way and then the other. He stared at the ceiling and tears began to roll down his cheeks, and his hands trembled on the arms of his chair. Wanda and her dad had been very close. The father's watery eyes saw no light on this dismal day.

To relieve the tension, Chester got up and walked into the next room. A very pretty young black woman lay motionless in the white casket. Her face was the very picture of peace. The detective wiped a tear from his eye and made her a silent promise to avenge her death. Chester signed the visitor's book and returned to the living room just as Mrs. Jennings came in.

"Mr. Brantley, here are the letters. You keep them as long as you like, but please bring them back when you are finished with them. She looked into his eyes and saw the sadness there. Mr. Brantley, I can see that you are a good man. I hope you get the man that did this. I hope you get him real good."

"Mrs. Jennings, I will do my very best to do just that. When this is over, I will come back to let you know. Would you like that?"

"Yes, sir, I sure would."

Chester bid the family goodbye and went out the door. He drove to his office and parked his car. He put the bundle of letters in the glove compartment and walked to Mack's place. Weary of puzzling over the case, Chester ordered a rum and coke for a change. People were beginning to get off work and drop by for a quick one on the way home. There were office girls and their bosses. There were a few soldiers and a sprinkling of lawyers and judges. Not to mention, the usual gathering of blue collar workers trying to ease some of the aches and pains of the day. Mack's place had a definite cosmopolitan flair. When quizzed, Mack revealed that Rita was coming in later. After finishing his second rum and Coke, Chester paid his check and stopped off at the post office to mail the skip report to the lawyer. He phoned the answering service from the corner drug store, but no dice. No new messages.

It was dark by the time Chester picked up his car and drove to the bungalow where Charles Pink lived. The bungalow was in the colored area. Chester parked the car in front. The entrance of the house was round at the top more of a portico. The Spanish influence was very visible in southern California. Chester could hear the throaty growl of a saxophone coming from inside the cottage. He knocked on the door and it swung open. The detective could see that the room was dark. He called out, "Charles?" Chester reached around the corner feeling for the light switch. Just then something heavy struck the detective behind the right ear. He staggered into the room trying to regain his equilibrium, failing that he sagged to the floor.

In his half conscious state, Chester found himself back in the South Pacific. Artillery shells were hitting all around him. Men were yelling and running. The ground was shaking with the force of the explosions. Rifles and machine guns were being fired. He was stumbling over bodies. It was dark and the explosions lit up the night. He felt bullets strike his body. Suddenly, he was jerked back to reality. He found himself on the floor in the darkened room. His head throbbed. He rubbed the lump behind his ear very carefully. He looked around the room, but was unable to see anything in the gloom. What was there about an empty dark room? You could feel the absence of life. He gradually raised his sluggish body to an erect position. He went back to the door in search of illumination. His knees felt like rubber. Finally, he found the switch and turned on the light. The room was a disaster. Furniture turned over, drawers dumped on the floor, papers thrown around the room. Someone had really given the room a going over. Chester picked up a chair to rest in. He found an empty place on the floor to put the chair and lowered his shaky body into it. The dazed detective realized he was covered with a cold sweat and his hands were shaking. War does awful things to a man's psyche. The light gave a sketchy yellow glow to the room. The detective rubbed the sweat out of his eyes and strained to see in the obscure light of the room. Then he saw him.

Across the room sat a young black man with a vacant look on his face. The man sported a red spot between his eyes and one little trickle of blood down his forehead. Charles would not be answering any questions today.

"Holy shit," Chester said to no one in particular. What information lay behind those unseeing eyes? "Damn it, I am too late everywhere I go."

Chester lit up a Lucky and sat thinking. He did not feel like answering questions all night. He snuffed his cigarette on the bare wooden floor and scattered the ashes with his shoe. Then he put the butt in his coat pocket. Slowly the ailing detective rose from the chair, but had to sit back down because he was getting dizzy. I can't afford to pass out again, he thought.

Gazing at the rubble of the room, Chester realized the killer was looking for something or trying to cover up something.

Slowly Chester rose once more. He wiped down the chair with his handkerchief and put it back where he found it. Then he picked up his hat, and toddled toward the door. Chester wiped his finger prints off the light switch. The chill of the night air felt good against his face. He looked around the neighborhood to see whether anyone was paying any attention, and decided colored people mind their own business.

He climbed into his car and drove home. On the way he stopped at a corner phone booth and called the cops. He reported a fight in progress at Charles' bungalow, but did not give his name. Arriving at his apartment he undressed and reclined on his bed. He took a couple of aspirin and washed them down with Jack Daniels. Thinking made his head hurt worse, so he gave it up and went to sleep.

CHAPTER EIGHT

The sun crept silently through the blinds and across the bed
to the sleeping detective. Chester opened his eyes and looked
around the room to reassure himself that he was indeed safe
in his own bed. His head was clear and free of pain. His lower
back hurt, but that was not unusual. He popped his back and
went to the kitchen and started breakfast.

The coffee and eggs tasted good. He opened the paper
with the thought, let's see what the day shall bring. It took
Chester twenty minutes to find a blurb on the last page about
a colored man being murdered in Santa Ana the night before.
The detective lit the first Lucky of the day. He picked the little
bits of tobacco off his tongue, and dialed the barber shop.

Joe answered, "Barber shop."

"Joe, how are you this morning?"

"I'm doing good, Chester. How about yourself?"

"I have a lump on my head, but nothing to worry about.
Can you talk?"

"I am here alone. You can talk."

"Listen, Joe, Charles Pink was murdered last night. Keep
this under your hat, but I think it is safe to say that Sam,

Georgia, and Wanda were all killed by the same person or persons. I want you to be careful. It seems like everyone connected to Reggie in some way is ending up in the morgue. I want you to start carrying Sam's Smith and Wesson and call me if anything seems out of the ordinary. Will you do that for me?"

Joe didn't answer for a few seconds. "Chester, this is out of a radio show. I didn't see this development coming. Do you really think I am in danger."

"I hope not, Joe. People close to Reggie are dropping like flies. I've not figured out why, yet. Someone was looking for something at Charles' place. So, I want you to play it close to the vest. Don't talk about any of this to your customers. Also, are you sure you can trust your man from Santa Anita?"

"I feel secure that he is okay, Chester. I have known him for years."

"Okay, but just in case, let me do the talking."

"Oh, I forgot to tell you he is coming in for a haircut today at four. Would you like to meet him?"

"I sure would, Joe. I'll be there."

"Okay, Chester, I'll see you at four. You be careful, too."

Chester showered, shaved, and tried to wash the cares of the world out of his hair. He put on his new suit and tucked his forty five automatic under his arm. He drove to the office and called Charley.

When Charlie came on the line he said, "Chester, I have some information for you. Why don't I send it to you by my messenger?"

"I hate for you to go to that much trouble."

"It's no trouble, Chester. Will you be in your office for awhile?"

"Yeah, I will be here."

"The package will be there within the hour," Charley said.

Chester lit a Lucky and waited. The information is starting to come in, he thought. How many more bodies are going to be stacked up before this thing is over? Chester checked the answering service, however there were no new messages.

Chester's office door opened and a lady walked in. "May I help you, Ma'am?"

"I am looking for Chester Brantley. Is that you?"

"Yes, I am your man."

The woman was in her thirties with long brunette hair. She had the kind of figure that men dream of. Her dress was made to accent every curve, and she appeared to be aware of it. She walked with a studied sway across the floor to Chester's desk. "My name is Marion Cole and I need to hire a detective."

"Have a seat Miss Cole, or is it Mrs. Cole?"

"It is Mrs. and that is the problem."

Chester took out a legal pad and his fountain pen. "Can you be more specific, Mrs. Cole?

The lady sat down and leaned forward revealing too much cleavage. "I suspect my husband is seeing other women."

"Do you have any suspicion about who he is seeing?"

"Not really."

"Can you tell me why you feel that he is running around?"

"My husband is a salesman and he has taken to spending a great deal of time in Los Angeles. It seems like he wants to be there all the time, now."

"Does he still treat you in that special way?"

"You're getting kind of personal, Mr. Brantley."

"I beg your pardon, but this sort of thing is a very personal matter. I can advise you in these matters much better if I know why you feel that he is being unfaithful. Perhaps you would feel better just telling me in your own words."

The lady thought for a minute, and then decided to bare her story to him. "Arthur has been distant ever since he started staying in LA so much. He hasn't been as attentive when he is home either. A woman can sense these things by the way her husband acts and reacts. When he is with another woman it shows in a hundred different ways. Sometimes it is a look, or a touch, or a lack of communication."

"It sounds like you may have something here, but what do you want me to do?"

"I want you to follow him and check it out. I want you to see where he goes at night and where he stays. You can do that, can't you?"

"Of course, but it might be expensive."

"My husband makes good money and gives me a liberal allowance. Money is not a problem."

"Let me ask you what you will want to do if you do catch him?"

"I will get a divorce and make him pay through the nose. Why do you ask?"

"It has been my experience that often times the wife will take him back anyway. If you think you would want to take him back, I would suggest just confronting him without the investigation. Sometimes the erring spouse will straighten up. You save a lot of money and heartache."

"I'll not weaken, Mr. Brantley. Do you want the case or not?"

"When would you want me to start?"

"My husband will be going to LA this afternoon. I would want you to start today."

"I have a conflict Mrs. Cole. I am working on a case."

"I don't like to be pushy, Mr. Brantley, but I usually get my way. If I am right about my husband, you will be back in a couple of days. Then I can go to a lawyer. Here are five one hundred dollar bills for a retainer. Will that be enough to start?"

"You are most persuasive, Mrs. Cole, however, I can recommend a competent man for you."

The lady leaned toward Chester even more. Her breasts were stunning.

"I am sure I can make it worth your time, Mr. Brantley, to do this little thing for me."

Chester felt his blood pressure rise. This woman would not be denied. "If it is that important to you, Mrs. Cole, I will take care of it for you."

Chester gathered the information he needed including name, address, phone number, description of the husband, temporary address in Los Angeles and the make of his car, and license plate number. Before leaving, Mrs. Cole shook Chester's hand and held on to it much too long. He gave her a receipt for the retainer and walked her to the door."

Chester lit up a Lucky and watched her hips sway down the hall to the elevator. He could see the elevator boy's eyes bug out as she stepped into his little domain. Crazy dames, she wants to get even with her husband and throws herself at me, he thought. It appeared to be a well practiced way of dealing with men for her, too."

Chester closed the door, sat down, and poured himself two fingers of Jack Daniels. He took a sip of the drink and blew a smoke ring at the ceiling. He thought about the fact the lady never even asked what he charges. She offered him too much money, also.

The door opened and the courier from the paper walked in with an envelope. Chester signed his name and gave the boy a tip. He opened up the envelope and settled back for a nice read. Charley had been very through. The envelope contained press clippings, photos, a list of phone calls made by Reggie, press service releases concerning the bombings and even the navy ship sinking. Realizing this reading would take awhile, Chester called the delicatessen and ordered a sandwich delivered to his office. He lit up a Lucky and called a fellow gumshoe friend of his in Los Angeles.

"Terry, this is Chester Brantley. How's tricks?"

"Everything is Jake, Chester. How are things going out your way?"

"Between murders and bombings things are strictly copasetic."

Jerry replied, "Isn't that the truth. What's buzzin, cousin?"

"I have a case to sub out to you. It pays twenty bucks a day with a bonus if it closes quickly. How does that sound."

"I am up for it. What kind of case is it?"

"It's a divorce case, Terry. You just need to tail out a roving husband. Is it a deal?"

"Sure thing, Chester. I can use the business."

Chester gave the particulars to the jive talking detective over the phone and told him to report his findings back to him. As he hung up the phone the office door opened and the delivery boy brought in his lunch. He paid for the sandwich and tipped the boy.

The detective felt a sense of anticipation as he began reading the articles and reports. First he read the telephone log for Reggie's room. He had called Sam's house, and three other numbers in the Orange area. Charley had looked up the names for Chester. One call was to Wanda, another one was to Charles, and the third one was to a phone belonging to an Eddie Conner. Chester made a note of Mr. Conner's name and number. The detective took a minute to look up the address for Eddie Conner in the telephone directory. Next he read the report of Reggie's accident. The report said that he fell off the platform in front of the subway train. However, there were no witnesses to the accident. He was alone at the time of the incident. The article stated that Reggie had been in the Fighting Forty-ninth. According to the report Charley had provided, Reggie had been cashiered out of the army because of an injury. Chester read clippings about the bombings in Los Angeles. Numerous soldiers had been killed and some had been in the Forty-ninth.

The press release about the sinking of the naval ship said it was caused by faulty ordinance exploding below decks. Numerous sailors had perished in the explosion and sinking. The name of the ship was the USS Terrell. The ship was a navy cruiser.

As Chester pored over the clippings and reports the afternoon wore on. It was almost four o'clock when he checked the clock on the wall. Chester put the clippings back in the envelope and locked the office door as he left.

He walked down the hall to the elevator and took it down to the lobby. Chester entered the barber shop and waved to Joe. A tall, well built, middle aged man sat wrapped up in the barber chair.

"Colonel Stewart, this is a friend of mine, Chester Brantley."

The Colonel smiled and pulled his hand from under the chair cloth to shake hands with the detective.

"I am glad to meet you, Mr. Brantley. You have a military bearing, are you a veteran?"

"Yes, I am, Colonel."

"Were you in the South Pacific?"

"You're right again, Colonel Stewart."

"Well, I am very pleased to meet you."

Chester took a seat in one of the waiting chairs and Joe continued with the haircut. Joe went up the side of the colonel's head, high and tight, with the clippers. He put a guard on the clipper and cut the top. Then, he put shaving cream around the colonel's ears and shaved the outline. Joe turned the chair around to the mirror.

"How is that, Colonel?"

"Perfect, Joe, you made a sale."

"Colonel, I'm caught up, now. Can I buy you and Chester a drink in the backroom?"

The colonel replied with a smile, "A gentleman never refuses a drink."

The colonel put on his coat, and the three men walked into the back room. Chester pulled one of the waiting chairs

The Three Coffin Caper

into the room so that they would all have a seat. Joe placed three high ball glasses on the desk and poured three fingers of bourbon in each. Chester offered the Colonel a cigarette.

The Colonel said, "Don't mind if I do. The cigarette companies gave us loads of free cigarettes during the war. I guess they will stop that now."

Chester replied, "I wouldn't be surprised. Colonel Stewart, I am a private detective. I am looking into the death of a soldier and some of his family and I would like to ask you a few questions."

"I see. So, your coming into the barbershop when you did was not by chance."

"No, sir, it was not. However, Joe and I will understand, if you don't want to get involved."

"Mr. Brantley, Joe is my friend, if he thinks that I can help you I will be glad to try."

"I am glad you feel that way, Colonel. I don't know where to start." Chester took a sip of his drink and asked, "What do you think of these bombings?"

"It is a puzzle to me. It sounds like fifth columnists, but I don't understand why the activity would be localized in Los Angeles and Orange."

"That is exactly what I have been thinking," Chester replied.

Joe asked, "Ready for another one?"

Chester and the military man placed their glasses back on the desk where Joe could reach them.

"Well, here is the rub, Colonel. Joe's shine man, Sam, was killed in the first bombing here in Orange. Then, we discovered that Sam's son Private Reggie Lewis, was killed in an unusual accident in New York on the way home from the War. One by one, members of the family and Reggie's friends have been dying ever since. At least two of them were murders for sure."

The colonel looked shocked. He took another drink from his glass. "I knew about Sam, but this news about his family . . . I had no idea. Well, this certainly makes things much more personal, doesn't it?"

"Yes, it does. Another thing that doesn't make sense is the fact that Reggie complained that he was just peeling potatoes and loading trucks, then all of the sudden he claimed he was working on something secret."

"This is mind boggling, but what can I do to help you, Mr. Brantley?"

"I am coming to that, Colonel, but I wanted you to understand why I am getting involved. I would like for you to make discrete inquiries into Reggie's service record and his duty. I wouldn't want you to stick your neck out."

"I think I can do that for you. Is there anything else I can do?"

"First of all, I would like to get your take on this explosion that sunk the Terrell. The news release said it was a case of faulty ordinance exploding below decks and sinking the ship. Does that sort of thing happen?"

"Chester, I'm not a navy man, as you know. However, I can tell you that rarely ordinance is faulty and goes off at the wrong time. This is the first time I have heard of it sinking a ship. You see, Chester, the navy takes steps to ensure that does not happen. They put explosives in certain closed compartments. That way if something happens, the damage is minimized. The news report said that the ship had been in port for a period of time. That is another thing that is unusual. Normally, you unload ordinance from a ship right away when you hit port."

"What you say makes good sense, Colonel Stewart. Do you still think you can check out Reggie's duty and his reason for discharge?"

"I believe I can do that for you. What unit was he in?"

The detective replied, "The Fighting Forty-ninth. It would be interesting to know where they were serving. I understand it was somewhere in Europe. There is one other thing. Colonel, you can tell me to mind my own business, but I am curious. Are you the commanding officer at the barracks? I know loose lips sink ships, but I have a reason for asking."

"I am the CO in name only since General Huff commandeered my command."

"What do you think of this General Huff?"

"I would rather not say."

Chester replied, "I take it he is not well liked." The detective watched Colonel Stewart closely for a reaction.

"The men hate his guts, Chester. He has them on forced marches and maneuvers constantly. The command is under manned almost constantly. He brought his own MPs and just took over. Portions of the base are off limits even to me."

"Seriously? He is keeping you out?"

Realizing, he was revealing such strong emotions, the general paused to regain his composure. "Perhaps I am being petty about the whole thing."

Chester tried again to get the officer to open up. "Colonel Stewart, this may be important. The bombings and numerous other deaths appear to be connected in some way to the army. I guarantee you that whatever you say will not leave the room. Now, please be open with me about your concerns."

The general sipped his drink and set down the glass with resignation. "Yes, there are areas on the base that I am unable to enter, now."

"Do you have any idea what goes on in those areas?"

"Chester, there is one area under armed guard with a number of troop trucks in it."

"Did the general offer any reason for the stepped up security?"

"He merely said that it is top secret. Chester, let me remind you that I have been far too open in discussing these matters."

"Not to worry, sir. As far as I am concerned, this conversation never happened."

"Thank you, Chester. Do you have a card? I will call you with the information about Sam's son."

Chester brought out a card and wrote Reggie's name on the back of it. "You can call me anytime, sir. If I am not in, the answering service will pick up. I hope you didn't mind my asking for your help."

"No, of course not, Chester. This is serious business and it must be stopped. As soon as I find out something, I will call you."

The three men finished their drinks and their smokes, before going their separate ways. Joe caught another customer and went back to cutting hair. The colonel left, and Chester returned to his office. He picked up Charley's envelope and his hat, before driving home.

When the detective stepped on to the porch, he could see that the front door was open. Silently, Chester pulled out his .45 and listened intently for any sound or movement. He would not take any chances this time. He waited a full minute before entering. It seemed like forever. He reached around the door to the light switch and flicked it on with poised gun. The room had been tossed very much like that of Charles. Sifted piles of junk were everywhere. After assuring himself that he was alone Chester stepped to the desk. Georgia's little packet of letters from Reggie was missing. So that is what they are after. I should have seen this coming.

Chester picked up the phone and dialed the barber shop. "Joe, I'm glad I caught you. Listen, someone tossed my place good and took some letters I had here from Reggie. Do you know anyone named Eddie Conner?"

"No, I don't think so, Chester. Are you okay?"

"I'm fine. Reggie called a phone number belonging to an Eddie Conner. You might ask some of Sam's friends if they know who it is. I suspect Eddie could be in danger, too. Keep that Smith and Wesson with you. Okay?"

"Will do, Chester. If I find out anything, I'll call you."

"Okay, Joe, I will talk to you tomorrow."

Chester got back in his car and drove back downtown. His digs were not fit for occupation. He drove around a few minutes to make sure he was not being followed. The detective checked into the Howard Hotel under an assumed name. He used the lobby payphone to call Rita at Mack's place in order to invite her up for the evening. He would feel better if she were close enough to watch. She said, she would be up around eleven. He placed another call to Eddie Conner's number, but there was no answer. The detective ate supper in the hotel coffee shop. He bought a razor and a few things in the gift shop and went to his room.

Chester turned on the radio. The "Amos and Andy" show was on. He sat down at the little desk in the room and looked over the clippings Charley had sent him. Even though he had a great deal on his mind, he laughed at the antics of the King Fish and Andy. The detective called down to the desk and asked for the bell hop. He sent him to the corner liquor store for a fifth of Jack and some mixers. The bellman returned within a few minutes and received his tip. Chester used one of the glasses in the room to mix a stiff one. He sat down in the easy chair to think over the things the Colonel had said. I would give anything to check out those guarded areas at the barracks, he thought. Those areas might just as well be on the moon, or maybe not. The detective dozed off in the chair and awakened to a knock at the door.

Chester went to the door with his hand on his revolver. He opened the door a crack and found Rita smiling at him. He dropped his hand from the gun and let her in. The lovers kissed a hello.

"Have you eaten, Angel?"

"Yes, I ate at the bar. Why are we up here?"

"Let me make you a drink, Lover. I have a lot to tell you."

Chester explained about Charles, the break in at the detective's apartment, and the changes at the barracks, effectively bringing her up to speed on the case.

"Good grief, Chester. This is beginning to sound dangerous."

"Of course it's dangerous, Rita. I wouldn't be telling you all the gory details, but I want you to be careful. I don't think you are in any danger, but people are dropping dead all around me on this case. I guess I am getting a little paranoid."

"Are we hiding out up here?"

"Not really. My place is not livable right now and I wanted to be with you. So, here we are."

"What do you think these people are looking for, Chester?"

"It's my guess that Reggie saw or heard something while he was in the army. I think he was killed to shut him up. Then the killers killed his father, mother, girlfriend, and his best friend to make sure Reggie had not told them anything."

"Then why search your place? I don't understand."

"I have been asking questions and nosing around into the deaths. In fact, I had some letters at my place that I borrowed from Sam's house. They were letters from Reggie to his mother. He mentioned working on something secret in the army. I think that is the key to the whole thing. The murderer wrecked Charles Pink's house looking for something. I would bet it was letters."

"Chester, for God's sake, you have to go to the authorities with this."

"I don't have enough to go to them, yet."

"What can we do?"

"We can be careful to begin with. Then I, not us, can keep investigating."

"Don't you think I am involved, now?"

"Not really, Angel, I just want to make sure nothing happens to you on the periphery of this mess. However, it might be a good idea not to be seen in public with me for awhile."

"Chester, you are scaring me."

"It is a good idea at times like this to be scared smart. We just don't want to be scared stupid. Do you see what I mean?"

"I would like for you to spell it out for me. I am not used to this sort of thing."

Chester scratched his head and said, "Okay, for one thing, be leery of soldiers until this is over. Wanda Jennings was seen talking to a man who may be a soldier the night she was killed."

"You don't really think the army is behind all this do you?"

"It could be a person or persons in the army. Wearing a uniform doesn't make you honest. So, just don't get yourself in a compromising position with a man in uniform or a soldier in civvies."

Rita shook her head, "Wow, Chester, this is just too much."

"I am sorry about this, Rita. I probably should not have told you all this. But, like I said, I want to warn you to watch out. I couldn't take it if anything happened to you."

Rita came to Chester and kissed him. He eased her back onto the bed. Rita pressed her body against his. Chester reached over and turned off the lamp.

CHAPTER NINE

Morning found Chester sitting in the easy chair looking out his hotel room window. Rita was in a deep sleep on the bed. He lit a Lucky and gazed at the scattered cars and strollers on the street. Wednesday morning was off to a start. The detective decided to have breakfast in the coffee shop. He dressed quietly to avoid disturbing Rita. On the way to breakfast, he bought a paper and a pack of smokes. The waitress motioned to a small table at the front of the coffee shop. The detective ordered sausage and pancakes. He perused the paper for scuttlebutt on the bombings. There were the usual stories about possible German groups and sabotage. The senate was setting up a committee to study the matter. The FBI was not talking. The president called for confidence in the government. The press said that many German Americans were being questioned. The taxpayers must be putting the pressure on their elected leaders thought Chester.

On page four a headline grabbed Chester's attention. "Private Investigator Dies at Big Sur." Little pinpricks of dread began to sting Chester's neck. The story was all there. Terry Foster, a local private investigator, ran his car off the road at Big Sur. The accident occurred about midnight when there was little traffic. The car crashed and burned at the foot of the high bluff.

Chester cancelled his food order and went back to his room. He would have a liquid breakfast. He poured himself a drink and sat down. He held his hand up and saw the fingers shaking. After the first drink the fingers did not shake as much. He put his hand over his eyes. Chester knew Terry's accident was intended for him. He went to his coat and searched for Mrs. Cole's information. He found the sheet of paper with her address and phone number. Not wanting to be overheard by the hotel operator, he went back to the lobby and dialed the number.

"Gramercy Hotel, can I help you?"

Chester replied, "Do you have a Mrs. Cole registered there."

"One minute please. No, sir, we do not."

"Have you ever had a Mrs. Cole registered there?"

"Not recently, sir. Perhaps you could try a different hotel."

"Never mind operator, thank you."

That proved it. It was a setup and poor Terry got caught in the middle. Chester felt a knot in the pit of his stomach. In his dreams people were getting killed in Okinawa and when he was awake they were getting killed in California. Chester lit a cigarette and dialed the answering service. He picked tobacco bits off his tongue while he waited for the operator to answer. Terry had left a message saying he was on the job tailing Arthur Cole. Terry would not be tailing anymore wayward husbands. Chester dropped another nickel for information.

He got the number of the hotel Mr. Cole was using. It seems that Mr. Cole checked out during the night. There was one more lead to follow. The dame claiming to be Mrs. Cole had given Chester her husband's license plate number. Chester called a clerk friend at the department of motor vehicles. A few minutes later the clerk rang the phone booth back to say the plate belonged to a car at the wrecking yard.

The whole thing was a setup, with phony names, phone numbers, and license plates. Someone wanted Chester dead bad enough to go to a lot of trouble. If the detective could find this cheap dame he could slap some information out of her. Maybe even solve the whole mystery of the bombings. Everything seemed to be a dead end though. He thought about the phony Mrs. Cole. She might have a record, but probably not. She was too flashy for an office girl. She looked more like an actress or a model. Maybe there was a chance he could trace her down that way. He remembered her long graceful legs and that statuesque walk. Maybe just maybe that would work.

Chester ordered sandwiches and sodas, and carried them back to the room. Rita was lounging on the bed.

He said, "Are you up for a sandwich, Beautiful?"

"You read my mind," Rita replied.

Chester and Rita ate silently. Chester lit a cigarette for both of them. The detective smiled at Rita, "Do you work today, Gorgeous?"

"No, I am off today and tomorrow. Why, what did you have in mind, sailor?"

"I thought maybe we could stay here for a day or two."

Rita stiffened. "Do we need to hide out?"

"Of course not, Angel. I just want you all to myself."

"I can never tell when you are lying, Chester."

"Okay, maybe a little of both. My place is all torn up and we could use a change of scenery. Think of it, Sweetheart. You can order room service."

Rita smiled, "You know I can't resist room service."

"Then it's a deal. I need to run by the office. Do you want me to run by your place to pick up a few things?"

"Give me a few minutes and I will go with you."

Rita jumped in the shower and Chester sat down and rubbed the back of his head vigorously. It would not do to let Rita know someone tried to kill him last night.

Chester parked in the parking lot behind his building, and left Rita in the car while he dashed in. He went upstairs the back way. With gun in hand he opened the office door. Just as he expected, the office was a shambles. He checked the lock and found pick marks. The detective locked the door and went down to the barber shop. Joe the barber was reading the paper.

"Hey, Chester. How are you today?"

"Joe, I want you to be very careful. Someone tried to set me up last night."

"Who?"

"That is the question? So, be on your guard. I doubt that anyone will bother you, but don't take any chances. Okay?"

"I'll be careful."

"Are you packing?"

"Yeah, I took your advice." Joe, indicated the gun was in the drawer in the backbar.

"Joe, can you do something else for me?"

"Anything, Chester."

"Will you call Pearl, the building maid, and have her clean up my office and my apartment? They both look like someone took a wrecking ball to them. She has cleaned for me before, but this will take a lot of work. Here give her this twenty and here is my extra set of keys. Ask her to get it done ASAP, okay?"

"No problem, Chester, I'll call her right now."

Chester smiled at his friend and walked back to the car. He took a quick look around, but saw nothing unusual.

"Next stop is your place, Beautiful."

Rita hooked her arm around Chester's. The detective's car purred as they glided up to Rita's place. The lovers walked in arm in arm. Chester breathed a sigh of relief when he saw everything was in order. He resisted the temptation to look under the bed and behind the furniture for intruders. Rita chose dresses, makeup, a negligee, and under things.

"I am ready, Sweet Prince."

"Then we are away, me lady."

Chester and Rita returned to the room to find the bed made. Rita smiled, "My, isn't this nice. You just go out for awhile and the bed makes itself. I could grow to like that."

Chester called down to the desk to let them know he would be staying a couple of more days. He poured himself a drink and sat down to watch Rita put away her things. She hummed as she hung up her dresses and laid out her makeup. She sat at the vanity to put on her war paint."

Finishing up, she turned to Chester, "As Mae West says, I feel like a new man."

Chester laughed and leaned over to kiss her. "You look so good it makes me want to mess you up."

Rita gave him a coy look and said, "That can be arranged."

"Before we get too carried away I want to ask you. Do you have any connections with modeling agencies or actors agents?"

"My friend Stella does. She models and tries her hand at acting from time to time. Why do you ask?"

"I am doing a trace on a lady that looks like a model or actress to me. Do they have books like mug shot books? I would like to take a look at some to see if I can ID her."

"I could call my friend. Do you want me to do it now?"

"Sure, why not?"

Rita placed a call to Stella. "Hey, girl, this is Rita. What are you up to?"

The girls chatted on for awhile. After a few minutes Rita said, "Stella, I need to ask you a favor. Do you have access to books that show pictures of models and actresses? I have a friend that wants to hire one, but he wants to look over the merchandise first. If you know what I mean? Okay, sure that would be fine. What time do you want to meet? I understand, I'll call you back about five. Have a great day."

"Chester, she thinks she can borrow the books from her agency. She says it has pictures of girls from here to LA. I can call her back at five to make sure she was able to get them."

"Good, now come here and show me what a good kisser you are."

Rita, climbed into the detective's lap and kissed him long and hard. The lovers spent an hour messing up Rita's make up. Then Chester suggested seeing an afternoon movie. On the way to the movie, Chester stopped at Jerry's Garage.

"Jerry, how's tricks?"

"I can't complain, no one would listen," Jerry said with a laugh. "What can I do for you, Chester?"

"Jerry, I would like to get my car lubricated. Do you have a loaner I can drive."

"Sure, you can drive the Merc."

"I would like to use that Mercury for a couple of days, Jerry. I am following a guy who knows what my car looks like. I can kick in a few extra bucks."

"Okay, Chester, I owe you one anyway. You helped me find my sister when she ran off. Your car will be ready when you are."

"Thanks, Jerry."

Chester traded keys with Jerry, and told Rita they were swapping cars. The Merc was in pretty good shape and the motor sounded good. Chester drove to the theater and parked. "Anchors Away" with Frank Sinatra was playing. Rita squealed with delight. It seems that Sinatra was one of her favorites. The lovers shared popcorn and sodas and wiled away the afternoon hours.

Returning to the hotel, Chester checked the service. No calls had come in. Rita called Stella and made an arrangement to come by the model's apartment at seven. Then she called room service and ordered a nice dinner for the two. The waiter set up the table for them and Chester signed the check. The table had red candles on it. Rita lit the candles.

Chester offered, "I would have ordered wine if I had known this would be so romantic."

"We can have wine when we get back from Stella's."

After dinner Rita refreshed her makeup and asked Chester, "How do I look?"

"Beautiful, as always."

Rita and Chester drove over to Huntington Beach where Stella lived. They took the steps two at a time. Stella met them at the door and ushered them in. She had the agency books laid out on the table and served drinks from a bar in the corner. Chester began perusing the books while the girls chatted. He turned page after page of lovely girls. When he finished the first book he opened another, and then another. Apparently the area held an unlimited number of beautiful young women. The drinks were good and the pictures of girls unlimited. Rita and Stella laughed and giggled and carried on like young girls all evening. It was late when Chester finished looking at the photos. He stood up and stretched popping his back. He lit a Lucky and turned to the girls reclining on the sofa.

They looked slightly tipsy. "Rita, it's after midnight. We had better go."

Stella asked with slurred tongue, "Did you find what you wanted?"

"No, I am afraid not. I couldn't find exactly the look I am after. Is this all the books there are?"

"That is all I have. I don't know where I could get anymore."

Rita said, "Thank you, Stella, we had a marvelous time."

Chester steadied Rita as they walked to the car. He put her in the passenger seat and looked around to make sure no one was watching the car. He drove around a little to make sure no one was following before going to the hotel.

He helped Rita undress and sat down to consider the next move. An idea occurred to him but it would wait until tomorrow. He put out the light and crawled into bed. Chester could hear sirens going somewhere in the night. More trouble, he thought.

CHAPTER TEN

Chester rose later than usual. The sun was higher in the sky. Looking out the eighth story window, he could see people going to work. His watch said seven-thirty. He felt discouraged because the evening's efforts had born no fruit. Chester slipped out and ate breakfast in the coffee shop. The detective checked the answering service and returned to the room. He scanned a newspaper he picked up in the lobby. The front page carried the story of still another bridge bombing. The Shoemaker Bridge in Los Angeles had been damaged by an explosion during the night.

Chester shook his head. He watched Rita sleep for awhile, and then decided to make some calls from the office. He left the sleeping beauty a note and drove to the Santa Fe building. On the way the detective decided to visit his friend at the gun shop.

Lloyd was behind the counter when Chester walked in. The detective smiled and shook the owner's hand.

"How the hell are you, buddy?"

Lloyd smiled warmly, "I am just getting older and uglier every day, Chester."

Chester replied, "So I see."

"Did you come by to insult an old friend or to make a purchase?"

Chester grinned, "A little of both, I guess. Do you have any good Colt .45 revolvers in stock?"

"I have four new ones in this case."

Lloyd took the four guns out of the case and laid them side by side in front of Chester. The detective tried each one and picked the one with the action he liked best.

"Do you have a shoulder holster for it and a box of hollow nose bullets?"

"No problem, Chester. Are you getting ready to start a war?"

"The way things have been going lately, we might have another war."

"God forbid," Lloyd replied.

Chester said, "That's right. God forbid."

The detective loaded his new purchase and put the holster on. He paid the bill and drove to the office. He parked the Mercury across the lot from where he usually parked. Then he went up the back way and entered his office carefully. Pearl had already cleaned up the place. What a relief. Chester locked and bolted the door, before putting both of his revolvers on the desk. He took the Los Angeles directory from a drawer and looked up theatrical booking agents. He took off his coat and went to work.

He dialed the first number. When the office girl answered, Chester said, "Yes, this is Timothy Johnson. A friend hired an actress to play a part in Orange a few days ago. I would like to use her for another gig. However, I don't know her name. Do you have any idea who she was?"

The girl asked, "Do you know what she looks like?"

"Yes, she is in her thirties with long brunette hair. She has a statuesque figure and walks like a model."

"Well, sir, most of our clients are under thirty. I can't imagine who the lady would be, and I don't know of any bookings for work in Orange lately. Perhaps you should try another agency."

Chester spent the day calling and getting the same kind of response. He ordered in a sandwich and a beer from the deli and kept at it all day long. Exhausted, he poured himself a drink and lit up a Lucky. Detective work must be ninety-nine percent sweat, he thought. Chester put on his coat and hat, and picked up his Colts before going down the back stairs. The detective took a long look around the parking lot before going to the Merc. Chester was beginning to like this car. It was a 41 Mercury painted black. It wasn't flashy but the interior was like new and the engine purred like a cat. He raised the hood. At first sight, he could tell Jerry had been working on the engine. No wonder it ran so good. The detective drove around for a few blocks to make sure he was not being followed before returning to the hotel. Chester decided to go by to see Jerry the mechanic. He pulled into the parking lot in front of the garage.

"How are things going, Jerry?"

"Fine, Chester. How about yourself? You know I like that Packard of yours."

"You do? I am beginning to get used to the Merc, too. You have done some work on that motor haven't you?"

"Yeah, it is a flathead V8, I bored it out, milled the heads, and put three deuces on it. I was going to race it until the war came along and put that dream on hold. Are you serious? Can we work a trade?"

"Maybe, is the Mercury dependable? In my line of work I need a car I can count on in a pinch?"

"Not to worry, my friend. I wouldn't steer you wrong."

"How would you want to trade, Jerry?"

"If you pay this little tab you have, we could trade straight across. How does that sound?"

"It's a deal. Let me get my things out." Chester walked over to the Packard in the stall. He opened the glove box and found Wanda's letters. He said aloud, "Oh, my God. I forgot about these." He put them in his pocket and pulled out the title and registration. Chester and Jerry signed the papers and the detective started to back out of the driveway.

Jerry came trotting up to the car window. "I forgot to show you the heater."

Chester quizzed, "What do you mean, the heater?"

Jerry said, "Here, I'll show you. Step out for a second."

Chester got out of the car with a confused look on his face. Jerry leaned the front seat forward.

Smiling he said, "The heater is right here."

He reached in and raised the cushion of the back seat to reveal a secret compartment with a sawed off shotgun in it. It even had a box of shells.

The detective whistled, "That is heat. Where did that come from?"

"This car used to belong to a cop. He had it made special. His wife sold me the car shotgun and all. I guess she got it in the divorce."

Chester grinned, "His loss, my gain."

Jerry laughed, "That's right, Buddy."

Chester circled around for a few minutes and then drove to the hotel.

When he entered the room, Rita was ordering room service. She was dressed up and looking very fetching.

"Hello, Handsome. What will you have for supper?"

"You do the honors, Angel."

Rita ordered steak for the two of them. Then Chester called down to the desk to ask the bell hop to get a bottle of wine from the corner liquor store. The two lovers enjoyed their repast and sweet repartee. The steaks warmed the stomach and the wine warmed the soul. Rita whipped up a luscious desert of kisses and caresses. Before long the lovers forgot about everything except each other.

CHAPTER ELEVEN

Chester awakened refreshed early the next morning. The sun was just beginning to break through the darkness. He lit a Lucky and turned on the desk lamp. He was anxious to read Wanda's letters. He went to his coat and took out the stack of letters. Once again he felt as if he were invading the private lives of others. The reluctant detective inhaled deeply and exhaled smoke at the ceiling. He opened the first letter and began reading. The letters were those of a lonely soldier away from home. They spoke of love, disappointment, homesickness, and hopes for the future. Reggie complained to Wanda about KP and loading trucks, too. He talked about how they would get married when he got out of the service. Chester read one letter after another searching for clues. Time passed and the sun came out. Chester read page after page. Then he found something. Reggie mentioned getting some sort of bonus and said he would be getting out of the Army soon. Reggie hinted that now they would have enough money to get married when he got home. Bonus? The Army doesn't pay bonuses. Where did Reggie get that stuff? That was the last of the letters. Chester knew he needed to follow up on the model agency angle and see Eddie Conner.

Rita yawned and stretched. "Hey, Lover, what time is it?"

"It's getting late. Check out time is in an hour."

"Holy cow, I have to work today."

"What time are you due in, Sweetheart?"

Rita frowned as she thought. "One this afternoon."

"Shall we stay at your house tonight?"

Rita's sweet smile touched the detective's heart. She looked as innocent as a high school girl when she said, "Of course, Chester, I love playing house with you."

Chester smiled and leaned over to give her a kiss. "We could eat an early lunch and then check out. I can drop you at work and pick you up when you get off. What time do you get off?"

"I get off at midnight, tonight."

"Then, that settles it. I'll get some work done at the office."

Chester kept up the pleasant patter with Rita at lunch. It would not do for her to know how concerned he was. They talked about how much fun they had been having together. After their lunch Rita got her things together while Chester paid the hotel bill. He dropped Rita off at work and cruised around before going to the office. He went up the back way again and locked his door after he entered. He placed Wanda's letters in a large envelope and addressed it to his Post Office Box. Chester checked the answering service, but there were no new messages. He spent the afternoon calling talent agencies in Los Angeles. The calls dragged on, one after the other, all afternoon to no avail. Finally, a helpful secretary told him about The Collier Agency that specialized in models that had a classic beauty and were a bit more mature. The detective called the number. He told the girl his usual story and she suggested he come to the office to check out their portfolios. She said they would be open till nine o'clock.

The traffic was bad, but Chester made good time to the Hollywood location. The office was tastefully decorated and the secretary was a knockout. Sticking with the story that he was looking to hire a model, the girl took him to a table with a stack of books. The detective lit a Lucky and kept looking for a couple of hours. At last, Chester found a photo that might match the woman who came to his office.

"I need to get this girl's phone number."

"I'm sorry, sir. That is privileged information. We never . . . ."

The detective interrupted the girl by waiving a twenty dollar bill in front of her. She took the twenty.

She remarked, "However, if you were to see her contact information on the back of the photo I wouldn't be responsible."

The girl turned and walked back to her desk. Chester pulled the photo out of the book and saw the information on the back. He pocketed the photo and left the office. He stopped at a filling station to call the model's number. Her name was Norma Ware. No one answered. The detective got directions to the girl's apartment from the station attendant. He drove to Miss Ware's apartment and parked on the adjoining street. Her doorway was dark. Chester stepped back from the door after knocking. He knocked again and waited. His heart beat faster in anticipation of what he might find behind the door. The apartment was as silent as a tomb. Reluctantly, the detective used his skeleton keys to open the door. He went in with gun drawn. He turned on the light and surveyed the room. Everything appeared to be in its place. Carefully he checked out the rest of the apartment. No one was home. There were numerous portrait photos of Miss Ware in the apartment. Apparently, she was the woman he was looking for. He snooped around, not knowing what he was looking for. In the bedroom the detective found clothes lying on the bed as though the model was getting ready to go out. He found an open purse on the chest of drawers. Chester looked inside to find her wallet and two hundred dollars in cash in it. That must be the price for setting up detectives now days. Her wallet contained her driver's license, social security card, and assorted female stuff. Why would a dame like this leave without her purse? In the bathroom Chester discovered a tub of water had been drawn. The water was cold.

The detective checked the apartment for signs of forced entry without success. On the way out he found two unopened papers by the front door. He had not noticed them in the dark when he arrived. The mailbox was by the door and contained several pieces of mail.

It sounded like a party was going on next door. Chester knocked on the door. A boozy broad came to the door. Chester could see a small crowd of people behind her in the living room and hear the moderately loud music.

The woman asked, "What can I do for you, bub?"

Chester asked the bleary eyed female, "Have you seen your neighbor on this side today?"

"That stuck up bitch? I haven't seen her for days."

"Can you tell me how many days?"

"I don't know, a couple of days, I guess. Why don't you come in and join the party, Handsome. I can show you a better time than her anytime."

"Do you mean to say, Miss Ware entertains men in her apartment?"

"If the shoe fits, buddy? She needs to put a revolving door on the joint."

"Do you have any idea where I can reach her?"

"Nope. Sure you won't come it?"

"Maybe another time," Chester replied. "Goodnight, ma'am. Oh, ma'am, do you know if Miss Ware owns a car?"

"No, honey, she rides the bus like the rest of us."

Chester returned to the car and drove back to Orange. He made it to Sam's Bar before midnight, and called Rita from the phone booth on the corner. He told her he would meet her in the parking lot when she was ready.

Rita greeted her lover with a big smile and a kiss. They stopped by the mail box in front of the drug store for Chester to mail himself the envelope containing Wanda's letters. He was not taking any chances. The detective explained that he had traded for the Mercury. Rita was surprised but pleased. They had a late meal at the all night diner.

"You had me going when you said to meet you in the back parking lot, Sweetheart. You're not getting ashamed of me, are you?"

Chester smiled, "Of course not, Gorgeous. Remember, I suggested that we not be seen together for awhile. This case has me leery, and I don't want anything to happen to you."

"I guess you're right. Do you have any good leads, yet?"

"A few, but who knows where they'll lead?"

The amorous couple finished their meal and went back to Rita's apartment. The day had been long and a night's rest was just the ticket.

CHAPTER TWELVE

Saturday morning broke with dazzling brilliance on southern California, shimmering in the presence of the Pacific coast. Chester picked up the paper on Rita's porch. He found the same kind of stories the press had been offering since the beginning of the bombings. The detective called the answering service to find that Joe the barber had left a message. Eddie Conner has been going out with a young woman named Dorothia Collins. There was a message from the M.E. requesting a return call, but it was too early to call. Chester made himself breakfast while Rita slept. He dressed and went by his apartment to pick up more clean clothes. He parked around the corner and walked back. Chester was alert for anyone watching. Everything looked normal as he approached the building. He entered his apartment with drawn gun. The room looked good. Pearl had done a good job. He got the things he needed and stopped off to leave his laundry on the way to the office.

The detective parked the Mercury and entered the Santa Fe building from the back. He fought the temptation to use himself for bait and just fight it out with the killer or killers. If he knew who to go after, he could save himself a lot of trouble. Maybe something would break soon. Chester was growing tired of being so vigilant. Just in case, Chester locked his office and placed both of his .45s on the desk. He called the M.E.'s office.

When the doctor came to the phone, Chester said, "Morning, doc, I got your message to call you."

"Yes, Chester, I received some information that I thought you would want to know about. A chemist has been checking out the remains of the bombings. He discovered what was used. It was composition B. That is a combination of RDX, TNT, and wax. You may have had some experience with composition B in the Army."

"Yes, I did. I was told dynamite was used."

"I know, Chester, but evidently that report was wrong."

"Everything seems to keep coming back to the Army, Doc."

"It beats me, Chester. I felt like you would want to know."

"You were right, doctor. I wanted to ask you if you have heard anything about a lady named Norma Ware. She is evidently among the missing."

"Is she from Orange?"

"No, she is from Hollywood."

"I will check it out for you. You think she will turn up dead?"

"I wouldn't be surprised, Herb."

"Okay, I'll let you know, Chester."

"Thanks, Herb."

The detective picked up the phone book and searched for Dorothia Collins. He wrote down her address and phone number. Chester picked up his hat and revolvers, and drove to the address. Miss Collins' street was narrow and the houses were small. Chester walked up to the door and knocked. No one answered. The detective walked around the house to the backyard and found a young black lady hanging up clothes.

Chester called out, "Dorothea?"

The girl turned around with a smile until she saw who had called her. With a frown on her face she said, "Who are you?"

Chester flashed her his badge and said, "I am looking for Eddie Conner. I understand you two are a number."

Dorothea looked concerned. The detective opened the little wooden gate that led into the yard. He walked up to the young woman. "It seems that Eddie has gone missing. When did you see him last?"

"I don't know what you are talking about."

"Miss Collins, there have been a number of sudden deaths recently. A number of Reggie Lewis' friends have met that fate. Eddie was a friend of Reggie's. Therefore, we would like to ask Eddie some questions. His life may be in danger, also. If you withhold information and something happens to Mr. Conner, you could find yourself in a great deal of trouble."

"Mister. I don't know nothing. I scarsely know the man. I haven't seen him in a long time." Dorothea picked up her clothes basket and hurried into the house.

Chester stood in the yard long enough to light a cigarette. Then he slowly walked away. His car was parked two houses down. He sat in the car and watched the house. A half hour later Miss Collins came out of the house dressed in different clothes. She seemed frantic as she got in the old car in the driveway. She backed out and drove down the street. Chester gave her a little lead and then pulled in behind her. The young woman was in a hurry, but easy to follow. The detective stayed back far enough to avoid her suspicion. She drove straight to Fullerton. She swung into the driveway of a rundown house in the colored neighborhood. She tried the door, and found it locked. She beat on the door frantically until a young black male came to the door. Chester could see the shocked look on his face when he saw Dorothea. He opened the screen door to let her in and looked around nervously.

The detective waited in the car. Shortly Dorothea came out in tears and drove away. Chester got out of the Mercury and walked between two houses to the alley. He slipped up to the back door of the house. He used his skeleton key to open the door, and slipped silently into the house. He could hear a radio in the next room. The detective eased up to the door and peaked in. The young man lay on a bed playing solitaire.

Chester walked in, "Play the red jack on the black queen, Eddie."

The man nearly jumped out of his skin. He started to run, but Chester blocked the way.

The detective said, "Don't try it. I can play rough."

"What do you want here?"

"Eddie, I need to ask you some questions. I might be able to save your life, too. So, take it easy and hear me out. I know you are hiding out, but I'm not the one you are hiding from. Here want a cigarette?"

Some of the panic left Eddie Conner's face. He took a cigarette and asked, "Who are you?"

"I'm Chester Brantley, a private detective. I am investigating Reggie's death and those of his family and friends. I know Reggie called you the night before he died."

"Whew, I thought you were here to kill me."

"I don't blame you for thinking that. Now, what did Reggie have to say when he called?"

"Well, sir, he said he did some secret work and made some money."

"Did he say what the work was?"

"No, he didn't"

"How much money did he say he made?"

"He said he got three hundred dollars."

"Who gave him the money?"

"The Army gave it to him."

"What else did he say, Eddie? Anything could be important."

"Honest that's all he said."

"Whose house is this, Eddie?"

"It is my aunt's house. I came here after someone killed Charles, and somebody tore up my place."

"Eddie, You need to lay low for awhile until I can figure this mess out. You could go to the police and tell them what you know. I have a contact in the department."

"No, sir. No police. I haven't done nothing."

"I know, Eddie, but I am thinking of your safety. If I can find you, they can find you."

"No, I will be all right. I will be fine. I'll stay here."

"Is there a phone here? I will call you when it's safe to come back."

Chester took the phone number and left Eddie to his card game. He drove back to Orange. The Army giving three hundred dollar bonuses just didn't gel. It sounded more like hush money. That is a lot of hush money. If that is what it was, it worked. Reggie was pretty closed mouth. Maybe someone didn't think he would keep quiet.

Chester picked up Rita and gave her a ride to work. "Have a good day at work, Angel."

"I will, Sexy. What are you up to this afternoon?"

"I am going to do some work at the office. I'll pick you up when you're ready. What time do you get off?"

"Can I call you at the office? I'm not sure."

"Of course, me lady. A pox upon me for a clumsy lout."

Rita laughed as she got out of the car. "Your fair lady will talk to you later."

Chester drove to the office. He went in the front door and walked directly to his office, locking the door behind him. The detective took off his coat and sat down at his desk, he lit up a Lucky and poured himself a drink. He took three pieces of typewriter paper with a carbon between them and rolled them into the typewriter. He paused for a moment before he began typing.

Chester typed the heading, "Report on the deaths of Reggie, Sam, and Georgia Lewis; Wanda Jennings, and Charles Pink." He double spaced down and began the report. The detective typed everything he had discovered about the deaths, and told about the letters and ransacked apartments. Chester told about the attempt on his life, and about tracking down Eddie Conner and the missing model. It took over an hour to include all the details. When he finished the report, he addressed three envelopes, one to Charley, the editor and one to Herb, the medical examiner, and one to Joe. Then he typed a letter to each man explaining that he wanted them to take action should anything happen to him.

Chester put stamps on the letters and dropped them down the mail chute in the office building on the way out. The detective walked to Mack's Bar and took his usual stool at the bar.

Rita looked surprised to see him, "What can I get for you, sailor?"

Chester smiled and ordered the usual. "How is your day going, Angel?"

"Fine, your boxer buddy is in the pool room. He was asking about you."

"Excellent, I'll see if I can find him."

Chester walked into the pool room and shook Jack's hand, "How are you doing, Jack?"

"I'm doing good, Chester. How about yourself?"

"I can't complain, my friend. Have you been knocking out anymore opponents?"

"Not lately."

"Join me for a drink at the bar?"

"I would be glad to, Chester."

The two men walked back to the bar and Chester asked Rita to bring Jack a drink. Chester and the corporal chatted for awhile. Finally, the detective got around to asking how things were going at Santa Anita.

"Oh, things are still crazy out there. The scuttlebutt has it that the colonel was shipped out. I guess this new general is here to stay."

Chester tried to mask his surprise. "Really, when did this happen?"

"The word is, he was called to Germany on a special mission for the general, yesterday?"

"So, he hasn't left yet?"

"They say he got on a plane yesterday."

Chester's heart started beating like a trip hammer. What did this mean? Is the colonel missing, now? He could feel his hands beginning to shake. The detective lit another Lucky and tried to conceal his discomposure. In his mind he could hear the rattle of machine guns and artillery explosions. With great effort he fought his way back to the present. He finished his drink and looked at the young soldier to see if he had noticed anything. Jack was busy ogling a blond across the room. Chester ordered another round and tried to calm down. He could feel his pulse slowing down to normal.

"Where's Flo tonight, Jack?"

"She had to work."

The two friends talked about women, duty stations, crazy officers, and numerous other things. Jack eventually got up to join his friends in the pool room.

"Jack, come back to see me before you go. I want to talk to you about something."

Chester sat at the bar thinking about the best way to handle his next step. He was running out of leads, and all the leads led to the same place. He knew he was running out of time. He couldn't kick the feeling of impending doom. If he made the wrong move, he would be in trouble. If he didn't make a move the trouble would catch up to him anyway.

Rita passed by. "I get off at midnight." Okay, Lover?"

Chester smiled, "I'll be here."

The detective checked his watch. It was ten o'clock. He watched Jack talking to his friends. When he looked Chester's way, the detective waved him over.

"Jack, let's take a walk around the block. It's hard to talk in here."

The two men walked out into the night air. "I want to ask you about something, Jack. I understand there are areas of the camp under armed guard. Is that right?"

"Yes, there are a couple of areas that I know of."

Chester asked, "Are there trucks in one of these areas?"

"Why, yes, there is. How did you know?"

"Can you get in there?"

"Not without being shot." said Jack.

"Well, we don't want to go that far."

"Is it possible to observe that area from a safe distance?"

"It's possible. I would have to think about it. Why are you asking, Chester?"

Chester explained the high points of his case and the deaths he had encountered along the way.

"Wow, Chester, this could be big."

"Jack, I can use your help and it might save some lives, but it could be dangerous. I want you to think it over, before you get involved."

Jack was lost in thought. He strolled beside Chester the rest of the way around the block. "Do you mind if I think it over till tomorrow night?"

"That's fine Jack, but please don't tell anybody what we discussed."

"You can depend on me, Chester."

Rita smiled when Chester returned to the bar. "I thought you ran off with the milk lady."

"No, Angel, I save all that running off for you. Do I have time for one more drink before you get off?"

"We should be able to manage that. Jack Daniels coming right up."

When Rita returned with his drink, Chester said, "Would you like to drive up to San Clemente tomorrow?"

"Darling, I would go anywhere with you."

"Rita, you are so adorable. You fascinate me. I would rather be with you than anyone else in the world."

"Save it for later, Sweetheart." Rita smiled and went back to work.

Chester sat lost in thought. This case must come to a head soon. The detective was tired of walking on egg shells. Something had to give. Chester needed a break and he knew it.

"Are you ready, Lover?" Rita had her jacket on and was ready to go.

"Of course," said Chester.

The two lovers walked together arm in arm. Rita didn't notice Chester checking to see if anyone was following them. They got in the Mercury and drove out of the lot. Chester drove around a little on the pretext of showing off his new car to Rita. When he was sure no one was behind them he drove to Rita's place.

Over cocktails Rita said, "Chester, you are different tonight."

"Different? In what way?"

"You are calmer, but sadder. You aren't about to do anything stupid, are you?"

"What gives you such crazy ideas, Lover?"

"Oh . . . I don't know. I just couldn't take it if anything happened to you, Chester."

"Rita, don't fret. Everything will be all right. I'm a big boy, now." Chester flashed his most charming smile at her.

"Let's go to bed, big boy. It's late."

Chester laughed, "My mother told me there would be girls like you."

CHAPTER THIRTEEN

It was Sunday morning and the lazy sun slowly climbed the California sky. Lovers slept entwined in each other's arms. Dogs barked for no particular reason. Cats stretched on the back fence. Church bells rang, but no one seemed to notice. Perhaps the day would be called for lack of interest. Half awake Chester and Rita cuddled in bed. Their bodies felt so good when they touched. The phone rang, but the lovers ignored it. They shared kisses and caresses. They inhaled the scent of each other and delighted in the taste of their kisses. In time they dozed in each other's arms once more. What a delightful way to greet the new day. At eleven they rose and shared a late breakfast.

After their repast they washed the dishes together. They dressed and drove down the coast to San Clemente. The Pacific sparkled a radiant blue. The white sands of the beach felt good under their bare feet. They put a blanket on the sand and talked of the good times they had spent together. They spoke of far away places they would like to see together. They talked about the way they met and how it seemed they had always been together. They looked deep into each other's eyes and saw the fire of love smoldering there.

Chester asked, "Did you say you have to be at work at seven tonight?"

"Yes, I suppose we should start back. I wish this day would never end though."

The detective acknowledged her statement with a kiss. "Okay, angel, back to the salt mines."

Chester and Rita showered and changed in the bath house and drove back up the coast highway. This day had been charming. Rita sat close to him as they drove up the road. The Mercury ran smoothly. Chester parked near the bar and they walked in together. He nursed a drink while he waited for his friend the corporal. In time Jack made his appearance. He took the barstool next to Chester and ordered a beer.

"How are you today, Jack?"

"I couldn't be better, Chester."

After they finished their drinks, Jack suggested they walk around the block together. When they were clear of the bar Jack asked, "Chester, do you think the Army is involved in all the trouble we are having?"

"Jack, I know it sounds fantastic, but a person or persons in the Army could be involved. Do you catch my drift?"

Jack walked in silence for a few minutes. "You may be right, Chester, but, what can we do?"

"I would love to give those trucks a going over. There is something suspicious about them. Do you know how many trucks are being guarded?

"No, I don't. I can show you how to climb up on top of the track building. From there we can watch the barracks with binoculars. Would that help?"

"Sure that would help. When can you show me?"

"Tomorrow night I could meet you at Mack's and we could ride out there together."

"That's a deal. What time?"

"Let's try seven o'clock, Chester."

"That will be fine, Jack. Come on, I'll buy you a beer."

The two friends sat together and had a couple of drinks. Chester warned the corporal to carefully plan their foray of the next evening. After Jack joined his friends, Chester sat at the bar talking to Rita.

"Sweetheart, if you don't mind, I think I will go home tonight."

Rita looked surprised. "Are you kidding?"

"No, Angel, I have to go home sometime." Chester gave her his most disarming smile.

"Okay, if you're sure, but I'll miss you"

"I'll give you a ride home, Beautiful."

"I'll take you up on that, Handsome."

Chester waited around for Rita to get off and then walked her to her apartment. When he was sure she was safe he bid her goodnight, and drove to his apartment. He cruised around the block watching for anything out of the ordinary. When he was satisfied he parked near the apartment. Chester pulled the shot gun out of the back seat and loaded it. Then he wrapped the shotgun in his coat and went to his door. He entered with the shotgun poised. Carefully he checked out the other rooms, and locked the door. The detective was careful to pull the drapes shut and stay away from the windows. Chester made up the bed to look like he was in it. He made a pot of coffee and sat a chair to the side of the room facing the door. With care he doctored his coffee just the way he liked it. The detective set an end table beside his chair for the coffee and ashtray. He lit a Lucky and placed the shotgun across his lap before turning off the light.

After awhile Chester's eyes adjusted to the dark. He became better able to see in the gloom. Time passed, he smoked half a pack of cigarettes and drank a pot of coffee. The detective needed to go to the bathroom. Chester got up and walked silently to the bath. He lit his lighter to illumine the way. Just as he finished washing his hands he heard the front door crash. He crept to the bathroom door as he heard the sound of shots. Chester could see the outline of a man in the doorway. He fired the pump shotgun twice into the figure, and watched the darkened shape blasted backward. The detective crouched down in case his assailant had a friend with him. The room was as silent as a tomb. After waiting an appropriate amount of time, Chester turned on the light. The intruder had two gaping holes in his chest, and a vacant look on his face. The detective checked the man's wallet and found a military ID card. There was something familiar about that face. Then he realized this was the MP that knocked Jack out. Chester called the police and waited for company. The neighbors gathered in little groups outside and talked in excited voices. When the police arrived Chester told his story and asked for Detective Logan. Logan arrived within the hour.

Eventually Logan took Chester downtown to make a statement. The detective brought the policeman up to date on most of the facts. At ten in the morning Chester signed his statement and went to Rita's place in an exhausted condition. He used his key and crawled into bed beside the slumbering beauty. What a night, he thought.

CHAPTER FOURTEEN

Chester slept until late in the afternoon. When he got the sleep out of his eyes, he found Rita had left. She must be working, he thought. He still felt like he had been in a gang fight. Chester lit a Lucky and called the answering service. He had received several calls from inquisitive reporters. The detective called the barber shop.

"Barber shop."

"Hey, Joe, how are you doing?"

"Chester, you made the afternoon edition of the paper. Are you hurt?"

"No, I am fine, just tired. I had to flush them out to prove there is an army connection to all the trouble."

"The paper didn't mention that, Chester. It just said you killed an intruder last night."

"Oh, shit. They're covering up. The guy I shot was an MP in the Army. Things are beginning to come to a head, Joe. Listen, rumor has it that the colonel has been shipped out. Is that possible?"

"Well, I don't know, Chester. I haven't heard a word, but it's too soon for him to come back for a haircut?"

"Do you have a phone number for him?"

Joe said, "Let me get it for you." In a moment Joe came back on the line. "Here is the number, Chester, Wilshire5-7557. Is there anything else I can do, Chester?"

"Not that I know of, Joe. Just be careful, these guys don't mind killing people. I will talk to you tomorrow."

Chester called Detective Logan at police headquarters.

"Homicide, Sergeant Logan."

"Yeah, this is Chester Brantley, did you get any sleep?"

"Precious little, Chester. How about yourself?"

"I got a few winks. Listen, I understand the papers didn't mention the Army. What's going on?"

"As we discussed before, Military Intelligence and the FBI are fighting over these bombings. This shooting last night will be hard for them to ignore, but they are playing it close to the vest. You don't have anything to worry about on this shooting. You will be no billed with the grand jury, and then you can have your shotgun back. I called it a riot gun in my report, so that no one would bitch about it being sawed off. I think you are on the right path with your investigation, but I want to remind you to be careful. Don't use yourself for bait anymore. Okay?"

"Thanks, Logan. I'll try to play it as safe as I can."

Chester thought for a minute, and then dialed the colonel's number.

"Colonel Stewart's residence, may I help you?"

"Yes, is the colonel in?"

"No, sir, I'm sorry, but Colonel Stewart is out of the country at this time. Would you like to leave a message?"

"Do you know when he is expected back?"

"No, sir, I don't? Would you like to leave a message, and I will have him call you when he returns?"

"That's okay, I'll call back later."

Chester lit a cigarette and called Mack's Bar. When Rita answered he said, "Am I in trouble?"

"You could say that. You had better get down here with flowers and hat in hand. Bye."

Chester mumbled, "Oh, boy." He rubbed the back of his head with his fingers briskly. The detective got up and went to the bathroom to shower and shave. He picked up flowers on the way to Mack's Bar. When Rita saw him enter with two dozen carnations, she smiled. She met him at the bar.

"Oh, Chester, they are beautiful. I can't stay mad at you, but I can't believe you didn't even tell me you had been in a gunfight."

"It wasn't a big thing."

"No, you just killed a guy is all."

Chester started to reply, but thought better of it. "Am I out of trouble yet?"

"I suppose so. You are making an old woman out of me."

Chester replied, "You are the best looking old woman I ever saw."

"Darling, I know you have a job to do and you are good at it. Just be careful. I have to get back to work. I'll get you a drink."

Rita put the carnations in a vase on the back bar and went back to waiting on customers. Chester lit up a Lucky and started going over in his mind the events of the last few days. The explosives used in the bombings turned out to be military explosives. Last night proved his point about the army or at least someone in the army being involved in the killings, and therefore in the bombings, too. Going to the authorities didn't seem to do much good either. Chester felt that somehow these trucks at Santa Anita were involved. Somehow he must find out what is in those trucks. The colonel leaving town so suddenly didn't make sense either. Chester checked his wrist watch. The time was almost seven. He looked around the bar for his friend Jack, but he had not arrived as yet.

Just then, a young soldier came up to Chester. "Mr. Brantley?"

"Yes, that's me. What can I do for you?"

"Hi, I'm a friend of Jack's. I have a message for you."

Chester smiled, "Okay, shoot."

"Jack said for you to meet him at the Roy's Café just down the road from the barracks. He will be waiting for you."

"Thanks, soldier. Can I buy you a drink?"

"No thanks, I have to meet friends down the street."

Chester finished his drink. He walked to the phone booth in the back of the bar and looked up Roy's Café in the book. He dialed the number and asked for Jack Turner.

"Hello, this is Jack. Who is this?"

"Jack, it's me Chester. What's up?"

"Oh, Chester, I knew I was running late and would miss the bus to town. So, I sent you a message and just came over here to wait for you."

"That will be fine, Jack. I'll be out there shortly. Let me pick you up outside. It might be better if we were not seen together near the barracks."

"Whatever you say, Chester."

The detective told Rita he had to run some errands and would be back later. Half an hour later, Chester pulled up by the café and Jack got in the car. The detective drove back the way he came.

"Aren't we going to Santa Anita?"

"I think we had better wait until later, Jack. It's still early."

"Yeah, you're right."

"Okay, Jack, what's the plan? Did you figure out the best way to do this?"

"Sure, when you think it is late enough, we will go up the fire escape on the main building of the track. From the top of the building we can see the barracks well. You know the barracks is set up in the parking lot. Do you have any binoculars, Chester?"

"Yes, I keep some in the trunk of the car. They come in handy in my line of work. Jack, have you had a look at these trucks?"

"Only from a distance. There are three two and a half ton troop trucks that are kept under guard night and day. The guards won't let anyone near them."

"Who are the guards? Do you know any of them?"

"No, sir, they are MPs that the general brought with him. They keep to themselves."

"Something tells me the General wants it that way, Jack. Here is a roadside bar. We can kill some time here."

The two friends went inside and Chester ordered drinks. They sat in a booth so they could talk.

"Jack, did you read the afternoon paper today?"

"No. Why?"

"I had a little run in last night with that MP that cold cocked you at Mack's Bar. He kicked the door of my apartment in and fired two bullets into my bed thinking I was in it."

Jack's mouth dropped open. "Wow! This is serious business."

"Yes, it is, Jack. A number of people have been killed already. I just want you to know what you are getting into. If you want to, you can just tell me how to get on that roof and not get involved yourself. I promise you, I won't hold it against you, if that is what you decide to do."

Jack finished his beer and Chester ordered another round.

Jack said, "Do you really think those trucks are connected to the bombings and the killings, Chester?"

"That is my gut level feeling, Jack, but I can't prove it. I have the feeling that if I can find out what is in those trucks, I will have the key to solve the whole thing. Another thing I wanted to ask you about, do you see the general coming and going from the barracks?"

"They keep us away from the barracks most of the time, but I have seen his staff car a few times."

"Do you have any idea what time the general leaves the base?"

"It's hard to say, Chester, but he is on the base almost every day."

"Yeah, that would make sense. He needs to run a tight ship. You haven't heard anything else about the colonel, have you?"

"It appears to me that something has to be done, Chester. I'm betting you are right about those trucks. If you are, then we have to do what we can to discover what is sitting in those trucks. It may be dangerous, but I didn't join the Army to play it safe."

"Okay, Jack, let's go take a look at those trucks."

The two friends walked out to the Mercury. They drove to a vacant lot adjacent to the Santa Anita Administration building. The area was very dark. It was lucky that there was no moon on this night. The two friends sat quietly in the car waiting for their eyes to grow accustomed to the dark. Chester got the binoculars out of his trunk. Then they walked quietly to the fire escape. Jack stood on Chester's shoulders to reach the ladder. He pulled it down so that they could reach it from the ground. The ladder squeaked as it rolled down. The two men stood silently in the dark to see if anyone noticed the sound. Hearing nothing, they crept up the ladder slowly to the roof. They climbed over the top of the building and sat on the roof with their backs to the wall.

So far so good, Chester thought. Silently they stole across the roof to the side facing the camp. Without speaking, Jack pointed to the north of their position. There under bright lights sat three army troop trucks. Around the trucks a make shift fence had been stretched. Two guards carrying M1s marched back and forth beside the trucks. The heavy vehicles stood to one side next to the fence. Chester watched the routine of the soldiers as they walked back and forth. They were obviously instructed to remain mobile. The detective watched to see if they ever changed their route in order to observe the other side of the trucks. At least while he observed them, they did not. Chester traced possible routes to the fence. He spent an hour watching and looking. Finally, he tapped Jack on the shoulder and pointed back to the ladder. Silently they crept back down the ladder, and made their way back to the car, after easing the ladder back up into normal position.

Chester started the car and drove back to the little bar they had visited earlier. The two friends ordered their drinks and sat at one of the booths. Jack broke the silence.

"What do you think, Chester?"

Chester lit a Lucky and exhaled smoke at the ceiling. "It can be done, but it's risky. I wish we could slip those guards a mickey, and just walk in there. We could give them ether, but that is a messy way of doing things. We could create a diversion and cut the fence while they were busy. Or we could just use stealth and hope for the best. This is going to take some thought. Why don't we call it a night and meet again. Are you free tomorrow night?"

"I can be. You call it, Chester."

"Are you sure you want to go all the way with this thing, Jack? If I am right, it could lead to an early grave. If I am wrong, it could lead to a court marshal."

"What is the best case scenario?"

"Don't do it for glory. The best case scenario is we would be heroes and the bombings, and killings would stop. But, let me tell you, Jack, being a hero isn't what it is trumped up to be. Let's meet tomorrow night at Mack's Bar and you think it over between now and then. Is that fair?"

Jack smiled and said, "Sure, Chester, can you give me a ride around to the gate?"

"Sure thing, are you ready to go?"

"Yeah, my bunk sounds pretty good about now."

Chester dropped off Jack and drove back to Mack's Bar in time to pick up Rita. He walked in the back door as she was closing the cash register.

"Are you ready, Sweetheart?"

"You've got perfect timing, Handsome. Give me a minute."

Chester sat at the bar while he waited. Today had been a fairly eventful day. If you counted his early morning visitor, it had been a very eventful day. On the way to her apartment, Rita tried to act like nothing had happened. Chester could see little worry lines around her eyes that revealed her concern.

"Hey, Beautiful, how was your day at work?"

"It was about the usual. How about you? Did you get any work done?"

"Not much, just some calls. Am I invited to stay the night?"

"I can't very well throw you out in the cold, Sailor," she said with a wry smile.

Over a cocktail the lovers cuddled in the living room. They were unusually distant on this night, both lost in their own thoughts. Chester was trying out different plans in his mind. Rita was rehearsing her concerns.

Finally, Rita, couldn't take it anymore. She blurted out, "Chester, you have to be careful."

The startled detective jumped, "What?"

Chester and Rita sat looking at each other. "I'm sorry, Rita."

"Chester, what would I do without you?"

"I hope you don't think I will you give you a lot of good ideas for a time like that," Chester said with a grin.

Rita took a mock swing at him. "Oh, you. You are hopeless."

"Honey, you know how I feel about you."

"Then why can't you say it?"

"Okay, you want to hear it? I love you, Rita. You excite me more than any woman ever has. You make my blood run hot. You call forth emotions in me I didn't know I had. You are the essence of me. You are my heart. Now, I have said it."

Rita sat on the couch looking deep into his eyes. Tears ran down her cheeks. Slowly her face turned to a sweet smile. She stroked his hand and swallowed hard.

"Rita, you are the scent of a spring rain. You are the sound of children at play. You are a cool breeze at the end of the hottest day of the year. In short you are everything that is good, and natural, and clean."

"Now, you have said it. Chester, I feel like I have always loved you. You are the key that unlocks all that is good in me. Kiss me, Darling."

Chester took her in his arms. He kissed her like he had never kissed her before. The world of trouble and cares melted in the heat of their embrace. Their hearts beat as one.

CHAPTER FIFTEEN

The morning dawned fresh and resplendent. Shafts of orange and yellow streaked across the sky, and outlined the clouds. Mockingbirds sang their song to the new day. The traffic hummed. Another day had begun.

Chester sat on the side of the bed and stretched. His lower back felt better than it had in a long time. He got up and made himself a nice breakfast. He called the answering service to check his calls. He had a message to call Charley.

It was too early to call, it would have to wait. Eggs and pancakes really hit the spot. The detective felt good about life for the first time in a long time. He turned on the kitchen radio, but kept the sound low to avoid waking Rita. He listened to the mellow tones of the Glenn Miller Orchestra as he ate. Those saxophones sound so smooth, he thought. The detective finished eating and dressed. He slung both .45s under his arms, and left Rita a note telling her he would talk to her later in the day.

Chester went by his apartment to get more clothes. The apartment manager had fixed the door and left a bill for ten dollars. The note threatened to send him packing, if the apartment was damaged again. Well, that worked out nicely, Chester told himself. He didn't even mention the two holes in the mattress.

He went by to drop off his dirty laundry and pick up the clean.

The detective drove to the office and walked in the front door. He waved at Joe as he went by. Joe waved back with the clippers in his hand and smiled. Chester took the elevator up to the second floor. He opened the door with his hand on one of his Colts. Seeing everything was fine, he smiled. Chester called Charley at the newspaper.

When the editor came to the phone he said, "What's up, Charley?"

"Morning, Chester, I understand you had some excitement this weekend."

"It wasn't too bad. You know what they say, any gunfight you can walk away from."

"Well, I see you are keeping your spirits up. I got your letter this morning. I am reading it, now. I take it you figured you were in for it, so you sent this just in case you didn't make it. Is that right?"

"Pretty much, Charley. However, I'm not out of the woods, yet. The guy I killed is working for someone who wants me dead. So, what I want you to do is be aware of the information I sent you. If something happens to me, I want you to force the authorities to do something."

"Your little problem Sunday night didn't get any reaction?"

"The cops still say it is out of their hands, and military intelligence and the FBI don't seem to see the situation the way I do. I still don't think they connect the local killings and the bombings. I outlined my reasoning in the report I sent you, but one thing is missing. The man I shot Sunday night was a MP and had his military ID card on him."

Charley said, "I see. Oh, I almost forgot the reason I called. I checked on the Fighting Forty-ninth for you. There have been a bunch of deaths lately and most them were the colored guys in the outfit. Does that mean anything?"

"It might, Charley. It just might. You'll see in my report, Reggie Lewis complained about KP and loading trucks. Then not long before he died, he said he was working on something secret. I believe he stumbled onto something while he was in the Army, and he was killed for it. Then the killers have been bumping off anyone they suspect he told about it. They are after me because I have been investigating. It just might be that Reggie and the other colored guys in his unit were loading trucks and discovered something, and they are meeting a similar fate. Now, there are some trucks loaded with something secret at the Santa Anita Barracks. They are under armed guard and off limits even to Colonel Stewart. Last night I found out, Colonel Stewart left town suddenly. I need to know what is in those trucks."

"This has the scent of a Pulitzer winning story to me. But, Chester, this is very dangerous. I doubt that we can get the authorities to act on it as it stands. They would say it is all supposition."

"I'm afraid you're right, Charley. We need to see what is in those trucks. I think they are the key to the whole thing. If something happens to me, I'm trusting you to find an angle to discover what is in those vehicles."

"Chester, you can count on me to do whatever I can. Just be careful."

"Don't worry, I will be extra careful. I don't want anything to happen to me either."

Chester hung up the phone and called the M.E.

"Herb, how are you today?"

"I'm doing well, Chester."

"You have been busy lately. I received your letter this morning. It makes interesting reading. I have your playmate from the other night down the hall. Would you say, it would be safe to assume this is all coming to a head."

"I hope so, Herb, but I need more proof. If something happens to me, I hope you can convince the powers that be to follow through."

"I hope it doesn't come to that, Chester. I would counsel caution at this point."

"I'm with you, Doc. So, just stay in touch, okay?"

"Sure, Chester, for your information the Army hasn't picked up your little friend. I contacted them to tell them we are holding the body. They would normally have responded by now."

"I understand what you are saying. Okay, Doc, take care of yourself."

"You, do the same, Chester. Oh, I almost forgot to tell you about Miss Ware, the woman you wanted me to check on."

"Did she show up in the morgue, Doc?"

"No, Chester, but I found out she is serving thirty days in Los Angeles County for prostitution. If you want to talk to her, I can arrange it. Just let me know when you want to see her."

"How would this afternoon be, Herb?"

"Sure, I have a friend at the jail. He will expect you. What time should I tell him to watch for you?"

"I will be there at two in the afternoon. How does that sound?"

"That will be fine, Chester. I will take care of it for you."

"Herb, I will need to see her in an interrogation room."

"I understand. No, problem. I hope you get the information you need."

"Thanks, Herb, I'll let you know how it works out."

The detective made some calls trying to trace a missing husband for Mrs. Janet Hill. He checked several of his best sources, and asked for a return call if anything showed up. He made himself a note concerning his progress.

Realizing it was close to noon, he grabbed his hat and went for lunch at Mack's. Rita wasn't on yet. He ordered a pastrami sandwich and bottle of beer. He thought about what tact to take with the model. Should he be tough, or easy going? Should he pretend to know more than he did?

When he finished with lunch, Chester decided to go ahead and leave for Los Angeles. He took his time driving to the Los Angeles County Jail. He drove by the girl's apartment on the way. It was a nice neighborhood for prostitution. He parked near a payphone, and looked up the phone number for the models apartment, the Carlton Arms. Chester dialed the number. When the girl answered, he asked for price to rent an apartment. Just as he suspected the rental was quite high. No wonder she had to turn tricks to make a living. Chester thanked the lady, and said he would have to think about it.

The detective got back in the car, and drove to the county jail. He gave his name to the desk sergeant.

"Yes, Mr. Brantley, we have been expecting you. Wait just a minute."

The sergeant came around the desk, and led Chester down the hall to an interrogation room.

The officer said, "I'm Herb's friend, Sergeant Winters, I'm glad to meet you."

The detective smiled and shook hands with the policeman.

"I appreciate your help, Sergeant Winters."

"I'm glad to help. This is a copy of the model's rap sheet. She has been busted four times for prostitution, and once for marijuana. She is known as a high class call girl, but even the ritzy ones get busted now and then."

"Has she ever been busted for the badger game, or extortion."

"No, Mr. Brantley, she hasn't been caught. That doesn't mean she hasn't dabbled in blackmail though."

"Okay, thanks a lot. Is this where I will question her?"

"Sure, I will bring her in anytime you are ready."

"I'm ready." Chester said.

Chester waited for his visitor. He lit a Lucky and waited patiently. Perhaps this would help him on the case. At the very least, it was worth a try.

The detective wanted to look into her eyes to satisfy himself that this was the right woman. Someone had taken Jerry's life in an effort to kill Chester, and someone needed to pay the price for it.

In a few minutes the sergeant returned and placed Miss Ware in the room. The statuesque model did not look as fetching in a grey jail dress. Her hair needed doing. Her fingers cried out for a manicure. She wore no makeup. Her eyes bore a somewhat glazed look. The model took a seat at the table across from Chester without being told. Her face showed no recognition. The detective offered her a cigarette. The hapless model took the cigarette, and Chester leaned in close to light it for her. He looked her directly in the eyes. Miss Ware was either a much better actress than he thought, or she really did not recognize him.

Chester said, "Miss Ware, how many times have you been arrested for prostitution?"

"You have my rap sheet. Read it for yourself."

"How many times have you been arrested for marijuana?"

"I told you to read my rap sheet, copper."

"Miss Ware, you aren't making this any easier on yourself. You are in a lot more trouble than you think. I will help you, if I can. However, if you stonewall me I won't raise a finger to help you."

The model sneered, "What do you think you have on me, flatfoot?"

"How about accessory to first degree murder?"

The model jumped to her feet. "What are you talking about? You're not penning a murder on me. Who are you talking about?"

Sit down Miss Ware. The model sat down slowly.

"Who got murdered?"

"A private eye from Orange named Chester Brantley?"

The model looked to the left. The name rang a bell. Then recognition dawned on her. But, a look of confusion won out.

Miss Ware said, "I don't understand. Wait a minute, you're Chester Brantley. You're not dead. What are you trying to pull?"

Chester said, "That's right, Norma, I'm not dead. But, that's not your fault. You set me up to be killed. The only reason I'm not dead, is I subbed out the case to a friend of mine. He is, or I should say was, a private eye in Los Angeles. Your playmates ran him off the road at Big Sur and killed him. You're in it up to your neck. You hired me to follow your nonexistent husband. You gave me a phony name for yourself and your make believe spouse, a phony plate number for his car, and the whole nine yards. They might even decide to stretch that pretty little neck of yours. There is no two ways about it. You had better give it to me straight. If you try to hold anything back, I'll see you swing for it."

"Wait a minute, I don't know anything about a killing. They told me you were giving this guy a hard time on a divorce case. I was hired to get you out of town so he could clear up his affairs. I don't know anything about this stuff. I swear it, I swear it."

Miss Ware broke down and began crying. Tears rolled down her face and she put her head down on the table. Chester slammed his open palm down on the table making a loud noise. The model jumped and raised her head up.

Chester said, "That won't gel. If you knew nothing about the killing why didn't you call the police when you saw the story in the newspaper?"

"I never saw any story about someone getting killed at Big Sur. I've been in jail since the day after I met you."

"How much did they pay you to set me up?" Chester yelled. "What's the price for getting a private eye killed?"

"Give it to me, Norma, give it all to me, or I'll turn you over to the hangman."

The frightened model's lip started quivering, "I swear, I swear, I didn't know what they were doing. I'll tell you everything I know. Oh, God, you've got to believe me. I'm a whore, but I'm no killer. Danny is the one you want. It's Danny."

"Who's Danny?"

Norma sighed, "Danny Martin, he's the guy that I work for."

"He's your pimp?"

"Yeah, yeah, you could call him that. He sets the calls for me. It's like a call girl service. It works kind of like an escort service. He makes the dates and I take care of the customers."

"What's that got to do with murder, Norma? Quit stalling. I swear I'll send you over, if you don't come clean. What else is Danny Martin into?"

"I don't know gambling, shy locking, prostitution that sort of thing."

"You've set up people for him before?"

"No, I swear. Give me a break."

"Finish the story, Norma, how did Danny get you to do this little job for him?"

"Okay, he called me the day before I met you. He said that he would pay me two hundred dollars to get you to go to Los

Angeles. He gave a little script to use along with the names, and the plate number."

"What was the story, Norma? What did he say the purpose of this little charade was?"

"Honest, like I told you before, he said a friend of his was getting a divorce and you had been following him. My job was to get you out of town, so the friend could hide out his mistress."

"Norma, you want me to accept that you believed this crook was telling you the truth? You didn't have any suspicions?"

"I thought you might be investigating some of his rackets, but I thought he was just trying to get you busy doing something else. It never occurred to me that he was trying to kill you. Why would he want to kill you? What did you ever do to him?"

Chester smiled, "Nothing, yet."

"Okay, Norma, I'm beginning to believe you. Now, where is this guy? Where do I find him? No stalling, give me all the information you have on this guy."

"He runs the Red Carpet Club on Brian Street. It's a nightclub, and he has a gaming room in back. Danny goes there most nights. He has an office where he can watch the club, and the gaming room through one way mirrors."

"How many men does he have working for him? He has two tough guys that hang out with him all the time. Moe is one of them and the other one Syl. Syl is short for Sylvester."

"What are their last names, Norma?"

"I don't know. I never heard their last names."

"Is Danny the boss, or does he work for someone else?"

"He and the other two guys talk about a guy named Blackie sometimes.'

"What did they say about this Blackie?"

"I can't really remember, but it sounded like he was important."

"Where is this Blackie from, and what is his last name."

"I don't think I heard his last name either, but I don't think he is too far away. I got the feeling he was close enough for them to go see him or vice versa."

"What else can you tell me? Give me something, Norma. You're not out of the woods, yet."

"Well, I don't know what else to say. I think he has a whole string of girls working for him. He gets them out of the modeling agencies. The girls need the money, because the modeling and acting jobs come in too slowly to make a living. It takes a lot money to compete in the modeling field. You need to keep your hair, nails, and clothes up in order to keep the jobs coming in. A lot of the girls take acting, singing, modeling lessons, too. So, the girls always need money."

"Okay, I get the picture. Now, what illegal stuff have you seen Danny doing? Have you seen him hurt anyone?"

"I haven't seen it, but I have heard that he has the boys rough you up, if you don't keep a date or you try to quit."

Chester remarked, "That figures, you are keeping nice company, Norma. Do they ever take pictures of you when you have a man over?"

"No, I might be a whore, but I'm not a blackmailer."

"What about Danny, is he a blackmailer?"

"Not that I know of. I Haven't heard any of the girls say anything like that."

"How about the gambling, do they play rough when the customers don't pay?"

Norma said, "I've heard rumors, but I never saw anything."

"Did he use you for a shill?"

"What does that mean?

"Did he tell you to bring your dates to the Red Carpet Club and get them to gamble?"

Norma bit her lip, "Yeah, he did. I can't get in trouble for that can I?"

Chester said, "Not as long as you keep telling me everything. If you hold out on me, I make no promises."

"I'm telling you straight. I haven't hidden anything."

Chester quizzed, "Okay, what about drugs? Are they into drugs?"

"They have a little marijuana around sometimes."

"Do they sell it?"

"I don't think so. Danny and the boys party with it sometimes."

"Norma, does Danny have dealings with service men? Does he make dates with service men for you girls?"

"Sometimes he sets us up with officers, and sometimes there have been stag parties."

"So he does deal with soldiers sometimes."

"Yeah, he does do a little business with them."

"Okay, Norma, let's go over it again."

Chester grilled Norma for a couple more hours without finding out anything new. He had hopes that he would be able to sweat something else out of her, but she was evidently being open with him.

"Okay, Norma, I feel like you are probably telling me the truth. Now, here is the deal. Don't contact Danny or any of his boys. By the time you get out of jail on this thirty day rap, they should be out of your hair. Then if you want to turn tricks you can go independent. But, if I find out you tip these guys off, I'm charging you, too. Besides that it isn't a good idea for them to know we talked. Don't worry they won't hear it from me."

"Okay, Mr. Brantley, I'm sorry about what happened to your friend."

"Keep your chin up, Norma. You're getting a break this time. Next time don't get yourself involved in anything this shady. Murder is a hard rap to beat."

"I understand what you are saying."

Chester went to the door and motioned for Sergeant Winters. Chester stepped out into the hall to talk to the officer.

"Sergeant, she spilled the beans to me. Is there any way you can keep her from using the phone for a few days."

"Yeah, sure I can put her on the no call list. I hope the info she gave you will help you."

"I hope so too. She seemed to be leveling with me. That is the important thing. You can put her back in her cell, and I'll take off."

"Okay, Mr. Brantley. Have a good day. Let me know if I can be of help. Tell Herb "hi" for me."

"I sure will. But, just call me Chester. Can I buy your lunch or something, Sarg?"

"Let's make it another time, Chester. Take care of yourself."

"Okay, Sarg, that's a deal."

Chester walked out of the county jail and up the street to a neighborhood bar. He ordered a Jack Daniels and lit a Lucky. It felt good to just relax for awhile. The afternoon was shot, but he had gained some interesting information.

Chester thought Norma was probably telling the truth. Gangsters like Danny often get women involved in serious trouble. Women like Miss Ware get trapped in a tough racket, and she is getting a bit too old to change. Chester thought about Danny and his henchmen. He thought about pressing charges. He knew it would be difficult to prove the Big Sur accident was really murder. Norma had no knowledge of a murder attempt, so she wouldn't help much in court. It was difficult for Chester to think objectively about the murder of his friend, but it had to be done. Unless he could get these hard cases to tell all, the courts wouldn't offer much satisfaction.

The detective knew there was a connection between Danny and whoever was behind the killings he was investigating. Probably Danny and his men had been hired to commit Chester's murder, but not the others. Chester needed to check out this Danny. He walked to the back of the bar and used the payphone booth. He put in a call to medical examiner in Orange.

When Herb came on the line he said, "Herb, this is Chester things went well here in Los Angeles, but I need to ask you another favor. Do you mind?"

"No problem, Chester, what can I do?"

"I need to check on a crook over here named Danny Martin. He's into girls, gambling, and who knows what? I would like to know what the police know about him. I would think he has some sort of record."

"Sure, Chester, I can check that out for you and call you back. What number can I use?"

"You can call me at this number, Herb, It is <u>AD</u>dison 5-5555. I will be around here for an hour or two."

"Okay, Chester, I'll try to get back to you as soon as I can. Take care of yourself."

"I will, Herb, Sergeant Winters sent you his best."

"Good, Chester, did he treat you well?"

"He couldn't have been better, Herb, thanks again."

"Glad to do it, Chester. Talk to you shortly."

"Okay, Doc."

Chester called Mack's Bar and asked for Rita.

"Hello, Beautiful, how is your day going?"

"I'm fine, Sailor, Is the fleet in? Will I see you tonight?"

"I'm not sure, Angel, I'm tracking down some leads here in Los Angeles. I'm not sure whether I'll stay overnight, or get back to Orange late. I called so you wouldn't worry."

"Okay, Sweetheart, take care of yourself. I'll save all my kisses for you. So, don't believe all those stories the other sailors tell."

Chester laughed, "Don't worry I know their just jealous. Goodbye, Angel." The detective was still smiling when he hung up the phone. Rita was always a lot of fun.

Chester ordered another drink, and lit up a Lucky. He considered his options. Herb would call soon with more information about Danny Martin. He could sniff around at the Red Carpet Club, and perhaps discover a lead on the killings. He could use himself as bait again, but that was always a daring way of dealing with things. He could come up with a story, and try to get the hoods to spill something.

The detective ordered his supper from the bar menu. The clock said it was six in the evening. It was too early to go to the Red Carpet Club, and Chester couldn't leave the bar until he heard from Herb. When the bartender brought his steak, he ordered another Jack Daniels.

Just as he finished eating the phone in the booth rang. Chester got up and walked to the phone.

"Hello."

Herb's voice said, "Is that you, Chester?"

"Yeah, it's me, Herb. Did you find out anything?"

"I got his rap sheet for you, Chester. His real name is Martino. He is from Chicago, and has had several scrapes with the law. He has been arrested for robbery, shy locking, assault, and suspicion of murder. Evidently, the law had trouble making the charges stick. The witnesses suddenly changed their testimony."

"Does his record list any known associates, Herb?"

"It doesn't say, Chester, but these thugs won't tell you much."

"Okay, Herb, thanks a lot for the information."

"These guys play rough, Ches. Watch out for yourself."

"I'll do that, Doc."

Chester finished his drink, and went to a movie down the block. He needed to waste a little time before going to the club. The movie was "The Horn Blows at Midnight" starring Jack Benny. The detective enjoyed the comic relief.

When the movie was over, Chester, grabbed a cab to avoid using his car, just in case. The cab driver was a cute brunette.

"Where to, Handsome?"

Chester smiled and said, "The Red Carpet Club on Brian Street."

"You must be a gambler." She said.

Chester replied, "Not so much. Why is the Red Carpet Club known for gambling?"

The little driver smiled and said, "You could say that, Handsome."

Chester suggested, "Why don't we stop for a drink on the way and you can tell me all about it. You can leave the meter running."

"You don't have to ask me more than once, good looking."

The cute cabbie, pulled into the parking lot of a bar and grill. She took off her uniform cap. Her form fitting khaki uniform was very fetching on her. The girl had nice curves, and a sweet smile. She would be hard for any man to resist.

Chester asked, "Do you go out with all your fairs?"

"No, I don't, Handsome, but you have to remember, there has been a war going on and all the guys are overseas."

Chester smiled, "Well, I know that is true. What's your name?"

"Joy is my name, what is yours?"

"I'm Chester Brantley and you are a joy. Come on, I'll buy you a drink or three."

Chester and Joy went into the bar and took a booth so they could talk. The waitress came by and got their order. Joy's outgoing smile was infectious.

Chester lit a Lucky and offered the pack to Joy. She took one and they both lit up. The waitress brought the drinks, and the detective paid for them.

"How long have you been driving a cab, Joy?"

"I started about three years ago. With all the men gone to the war, the girls had to pitch in. Some of my friends have been building planes, and driving trucks. So, I figured this was the least I could do."

The detective said, "I guess the guys will be coming back and the GI Bill will force the cab company to give them back their jobs."

"Yeah, it looks that way. But, I guess that is the way it should be."

"Joy, you are very charming. I have a feeling you will be alright no matter what happens."

"Chester, you are a charmer, too. How come you aren't in the Army?"

"I was, but I got shot up and sent home."

"Where are you from, Handsome?"

Chester replied, "I'm from Orange."

"I can't believe a man as good looking as you is living in Orange without me tracking you down."

"It isn't that bad, is it?"

Joy grinned, "Almost."

Chester smiled and asked, "What's the scoop on the Red Carpet Club?"

"I have taken a number of fairs there, and I have been there a few times. There is gambling in the back room. There are a bunch of hookers that go there, too. They sometimes try to get me to get them dates for a cut of the take. I don't get involved in that. That sort of thing is like a tar baby. You can't get out of it once you get in."

"You're smart too, Joy. That sort of thing can ruin a nice girl. What else can you tell me about the club?"

"Chester, are you a cop?"

"Joy, you are such a sweet kid I'm going to level with you, I'm a private detective. But, no I'm not a cop."

"I didn't think you were a cop, but you are very curious about this club."

"There is a reason for my curiosity. What else can you tell me?"

"Okay, the place is managed or owned or something by a guy named Danny Martin. He is kind of dark character. You wouldn't want to cross him. He has a couple of body guards that run with him all the time. They are just mussel, but they are tough guys."

"Joy, do have any knowledge of crimes they have committed?"

"Just hearsay, Chester. Some of the hookers have told me stories of beatings. That is outside of the gambling, it's illegal."

Chester inquired, "Do the hookers actually work in the club?"

"No, they are call girls, but they say they work for Danny, too."

Joy finished her drink and quizzed, "Can I ask what you are investigating, Chester. I'm all for law and order, maybe I can help."

"Can I trust you not to say anything about this, Joy?"

"I promise I won't say anything, Chester."

"Okay, I suspect that Danny was paid to run a friend of mine off the road in an effort to kill him."

"Oh, Chester, I'm sorry. Did they actually kill him?"

"Yes, they did."

"Oh, God, I knew those guys were bad news."

"Yeah, they are that for sure."

Joy asked, "What can I do to help, Chester?"

"You could be my date tonight. I would like to have a look around over there. With you with me, no one would pay me any attention."

Joy smiled, "You are such a charmer, Chester. I would love to go with you. We can stop at my apartment so I can change."

"Do you have to turn in the cab?"

"Yeah, but I have my own car. We can use it."

"What about work, Joy?"

"It's time for me to get off anyway. Come on let's go. It won't take long."

Chester paid Joy the money he owed her, and they drove to the cab company to turn in her unit. They picked up her Chevrolet and went by her apartment to let her change. Chester made himself a drink and lit a Lucky while he waited. The girl's apartment was as cute as she was. Joy had fixed it up real nice. She would make someone a great wife. The place was neat as a pen.

"Are you ready, Chester?"

"I am if you are."

"Okay, let's go. I want to show you off."

Joy drove to the Red Carpet Club and parked in back. The lot was packed. When they got inside, Chester checked Joy's coat and his hat. They made their way to the floor of the club. They were lucky to get a table, the place was full. The club had a large dance floor and a stage with a big band orchestra. The dancers were jitterbugging all over the floor. Someone spent some money to put in this place. When the waitress came by Chester ordered their drinks.

Joy smiled at the detective, "Let's dance, Chester."

The detective followed the curvy cab driver to the dance floor. They did the Lindy Hop.

When they returned to their seats Joy said, "You didn't tell me you could dance like that."

Chester smiled, "I can do a few things."

Joy smiled, "You are so much fun."

A singer came out and sang a few songs. She was a slender woman in an electric blue dress. She sang and danced around the stage putting on quite a show. Chester took it all in. After the singer finished her set, the band took over and the dancers took the floor again. Chester and Joy cut a rug. Joy was a better dancer than the detective, however he held his own.

After an hour or so Chester suggested, "Let's check out the gaming room."

"Okay, Chester."

Joy led the way up the stairs, and to a back room. A man opened a slot in the door. She smiled and in a second the man opened the door for them. Business was booming in the gaming room. There were numerous tables and they were all crowded. People were milling around, and yelling when they won. There was black jack, and roulette, craps, and slot machines. Chester bought some chips and they played for awhile. They played blackjack, roulette, and finally they played craps.

Chester said, "Shall we go back to the dance floor?"

"Okay, Chester."

They got another table and ordered another drink.

"Chester, what do you think of the gaming room?"

"The dealers are dealing seconds, the dice game appears to be honest, but I'm not sure about the roulette wheel. I think it might be crooked, too."

"Wow, I would think the house odds would be enough."

"It should be, Joy, but once a crook always a crook. They just have to tilt the odds in their favor. It isn't gambling the way they do it."

"I guess you're right, Chester."

"Have you seen Danny or his men tonight?"

"No, I haven't but they usually come in late. You'll know Danny. He'll have a couple of flashy girls with him and wearing a tux. He likes to put on the dog."

"Joy, do you know where Danny's office is."

"Yeah, it's right up there. See that mirror. His office is behind it. So, he can see the club. From the other side of the office he can see into the gaming room."

"Do you know which door he uses to come and go?"

"One of the girl's says he uses a back way."

Chester remarked, "That is probably in case the place gets raided. It wouldn't do for him to get arrested."

"Do you have any idea what time of night Danny leaves, or what kind of car he drives, Joy?"

"He drives a black Cadillac, but I'm not sure how late he stays. He probably stays till closing. I've heard he doesn't trust the employees.

"That could very well be true. No honor among thieves. I'll be back in a few minutes. I want to take a look around."

Chester went outside and lit a Lucky. He picked the tobacco bits off his tongue with his thumb and forefinger. Casually he walked around the building. He found a nice black Cadillac parked in a reserved parking space in the back. There was a back door close by. He tried the back door and found it locked. The detective continued walking all the way around the building, and back to the front.

Chester went back to the table. Joy smiled at him when he sat down. The detective ordered another round of drinks. He lit two cigarettes and gave one to Joy.

"Are you having fun, Joy?"

"I really am, Chester. You are a nice guy."

"I'm not as nice as you are, Joy. You really are special. I mean it."

As Chester and Joy talked they became aware of a change in the room. They looked around to see an Italian man walking through the club with a blonde on each arm. He was wearing a tux, and sporting the blonds like they were diamonds. It was obvious he wanted everyone to see what kind of merchandise he traveled with. The girls looked like models. They were probably part of his stable. Obviously this was Danny. He was flanked by two tough looking mugs. Danny stopped and greeted some of the guests. He was playing the role of a movie star instead of a thug. The guests of the club seemed to be buying the show. They smiled and waved at him.

Chester took the measure of the man, and found him lacking. The body guards looked fairly tough but short on brains. The detective's eyes followed the entourage as they made the rounds of the club and drifted up to the gambling room. Chester could see the door with the sliding peep hole from the table. He watched until they came out. The detective walked over to the cigarette girl and bought a pack of Lucky Strikes in order to keep an eye on where they went. He saw them enter a door that would be Danny's office.

Chester returned to his seat. "So that is Danny."

Joy smiled, "He's a hoot isn't he?"

Chester laughed, "He thinks he's George Raft or something. What time does this place close?"

"They stay open until four in the morning. I guess if you are going to have illegal gambling you might as well stay open past closing time, too."

Chester said, "Makes sense to me. Are you ready to go home? It's past midnight."

"It's probably a good idea. I have to work tomorrow."

Chester and Joy walked out to the car. Joy drove back toward her place.

Chester said, "Can you give me a ride back to where you picked me up?"

"Are you staying in a hotel there or something, Chester?"

"No, my car is parked there."

"Then why did you need a cab?" Joy said, perplexed.

"I was afraid our boys would recognize my car. You see they were supposed to kill me instead of my friend."

"Oh, my God. Really?"

"I'll take you to your car, Chester, but you have to promise me you will be careful."

"Don't worry, Joy. I'm extremely good at staying alive. I'm mainly just trying to find out who hired Danny to kill me. When I find that out, I can try to put a stop to it."

Joy drove back to the place where she picked up Chester and he directed her to where the Mercury was parked. They sat in the girl's car looking at each other.

"Chester, I really like you. If I give you my number will you call me?"

"Joy, I am seeing someone, but we don't have a stated relationship. I find you fascinating, but I'm sure all the other guys do, too. I would like to stay in touch and see you when I'm in town. How does that sound?"

"You really are a nice guy. That sounds fair to me. Can I have one of your cards?"

Chester smiled, "I would be glad to give you one, but I hope you won't need me professionally."

"Let's hope not, Chester."

The detective gave Joy a card and kissed her goodnight. She drove away and he got in the Mercury and drove back to the Red Carpet Club. He sat in the parking lot until three waiting for the crowd to thin out a little. By that time the lot was half empty.

Chester got out of the car and walked to the back door he had discovered earlier. He used his lock picks to open the door and went in. He found himself in the back of the kitchen. The place was deserted, but there was a light on. There was a hallway. The detective made his way down the hall to a stairway. This must lead up to Danny's office. Chester made his way up the steps as quietly as possible. At the top of the stairs he found a door. The detective drew one of his Colts and carefully tried the knob. It turned, the door was not locked. Chester eased the door open to find another darkened hall.

The detective slipped through the door and tried to get his bearings. He found another likely looking door and listened for any sound within. He was unable to detect anything. This door was locked, too. Chester picked the lock carefully and quietly, and eased it open. It was just a storage room. He walked further down the hall and heard someone coming. He slipped into another doorway and waited. He saw a man in a suit carrying a till. He was walking in the half light of the hallway from the other end. He stopped at a door on the other side of the passage, and knocked twice. There was a muffled "yeah" from within the room. "I've got a till, boss." The door opened and the man went in. Within a few minutes the man, probably a waiter, came out.

Chester stood silently in the hall until the man returned through the door he had entered. The detective waited a full two minutes. He drew his other colt and stepped to the door. He knocked twice as the other man had done. The detective's heart was pounding with excitement. From the room came a muffled "yeah". "I've got a till, boss." The door opened and Chester went in with both guns drawn.

Danny Martin sat at his desk counting money. He didn't look up at first. Chester gave the room a quick look. The guards weren't in the room. Danny looked up to see two .45 Colts pointed at him. His mouth dropped open. He seemed at a loss for words.

Finally, he found his tongue, "What's this? A hold up?"

"Keep your money, Danny. I want a bigger payoff."

"You mean you're a cop, and you want hush money."

"I mean you tried to kill me the other night, and I'm here to return the favor."

"A look of terror filled the gangster's face. He started to move one of his hands and thought better of it."

Chester commanded, "Get your hands up, Danny, and back that chair away from the desk. I wouldn't want you to touch any buttons or anything."

The cringing mobster pushed his chair back from the desk with his feet. He raised his shaking hands in the air. He looked confused and scared.

"Who are you?"

"I'm Chester Brantley. Does that ring any bells? You had better come across with the answers now or I'll plug you on the spot."

Danny replied, "Yeah, okay, what do you want to know."

"Just for the record, Danny, why did you try to kill me?"

"Oh . . . that was nothing personal. I don't even know you. I got nothing against you. That was just business."

"Spit it out, Danny, what business?"

Chester cocked back both hammers on the Colt .45s. Danny's eyes got even bigger. He was sweating profusely.

"Wait a minute. Wait a minute, Brantley. Take it easy. I got nothing against you. A guy paid me to do the job that's all. I swear it was just business."

"Give it to me, Danny, what guy hired you?"

"Some Army guy."

"What Army guy, I'm getting bored with you, Danny."

"I don't know. It was some Army officer. He had been in here gambling a few times. He was losing heavy. But, then he came up with the money and asked me to do a job. He gave me two thousand to create an accident for you. That's all it was for me just business. He didn't even get mad when we got the wrong guy. Yeah, you and I are quits. He didn't even ask us to try again."

"Who set it up, Danny, was it Blackie?"

"Blackie, how did you know about Blackie?"

"I've got the guns, Danny, I ask the questions. Now, answer the question."

"No, Blackie didn't even know about this till after the fact."

"So, you set up the whole thing."

"Well . . . well . . . I took the money, but it was only business. Like I say we are quits. I'm not after you. I don't bother you, you don't bother me. The war is over. We got a truce. That's okay isn't it? Why not? I don't bother you and you don't bother me. I don't even know what your beef with the Army is. Okay, big guy? Come on you want money, I got money. Whatever you say, I go my way and you go your way. We got no problems. I understand you got mad. But, let's handle this like businessmen. It was just bad business, but it's over now. Okay?"

Chester said, "What's behind that door?"

Danny replied, "Just a room to lock the tills in."

"Okay, open the door."

Danny got up from the chair with his hands still in the air, and backed to the door. "I got to get the keys out of my pocket. Okay?"

"Don't make any fast moves, or I'll mess up that nice suit of yours."

Danny's hands were still shaking. He slowly removed the key, and unlocked the door.

"Open the door, and stand to the side," said Chester."

Danny did what he was told. The room was dark, but the detective could see it was just a walkin closet with shelves for the tills.

"Get inside, Danny."

The gangster completely lost his nerve. "No, Brantley, no, don't do this."

"Calm down, Danny, I'm just going to lock you in till I'm gone."

The gangster was shaking violently. He could barely walk. He stepped into the room. Chester struck him behind the right ear and the cowardly gangster tumbled to the floor.

The detective locked the door, and went out the way he came in. He hurried down the darkened hall, and the stairway. He reached the outside door without being seen. The detective holstered his guns, and stepped out into the parking lot. Chester walked toward his car. He fought the impulse to run. His heart was beating like a base drum. He walked as calmly as he could. He even stopped to light a cigarette. Every fiber within his being wanted to be away from this place. He kept walking.

Suddenly, he heard a noise. He jerked around to look at the back door. There they stood, Danny and the two bodyguards with drawn guns. Chester ran to the closest car fighting to get his .45s out. Just as he got to the car, one of its headlights exploded. All bets were off they were out to kill him this time.

The detective ducked down beside the car, and looked up to see where they were. He saw one of them dashing across the lot. Chester fired at him, but missed. Another bullet hit the windshield beside the detective. He turned and fired in the direction the shot came from. One of the guards stood up, and fell backward. Without warning a hail of bullets began to strike the car the detective was using for a shield. Glass shattered, and lead thudded into metal.

Chester turned and in a crouching run ran around to the other side of the car. He waited silently for the gangsters to make their next move. He strained to see any movement. Then he saw the flash of a pistol, and he fired three shots directly at the source of the flash. He heard a groan, and the sound of a gun hitting the ground.

The detective called out. "That just leaves us now, Danny. What are you going to do, now? Have you got enough backbone to finish this?"

There was no response. Chester slowly rose to his feet. He felt that Danny was somewhere directly in front of him crouched behind one of those cars in the dark. The detective knew it was hard to shoot straight with shaky hands. Chester stood there waiting for the slightest sound or movement. He took a couple of steps making a better target of himself. Then, he heard the sound of a pistol being cocked. He fired four shots in the direction the sound came from. Danny screamed in agony, and then went quiet. The detective stood transfixed, but no more shots were forthcoming. Slowly Chester walked toward the spot he had fired at. When he got there he saw the crumpled figure of Danny with a growing puddle of blood. He looked at the gory sight and thought that's for you, Jerry.

Chester heard a siren and saw the flashing lights of the police car. He laid his pistols on the car and pulled out his badge and ID. When the car pulled up he held up the badge in plain view.

"What happened here?" said the officer.

"These gangsters tried to kill me. They just weren't good enough."

"Okay, these your guns?"

"Yeah."

"Oh, I know this guy, Danny Martin. A cheap hood, so he finally got his. Well, there won't be any tears shed over him. Let me see your ID, Chester Brantley. Okay, Chester, pick up your guns. When the lieutenant hears about this you might get a medal. Okay, Joe, call homicide."

Chester holstered his guns and said, "There are two more of them one over there, and one over there."

The officer replied, "Sounds like you really cleaned house tonight. Why were they trying to kill you?"

"The one you called Danny said someone paid him to kill me."

"It doesn't look like the guy got his money's worth."

Chester sat on the fender of a parked car waiting for homicide to arrive. He could hear more sirens screaming in the distance. They always reminded him of the war for some reason. In the distance he could hear the rattle of machine gun fire. He could feel the earth shaking. He could see soldiers running, and artillery exploding. The detective's hands began to shake.

Then Chester reached down within himself in an effort to overcome these visions of the past, to drive away the demons of war to still the hellhounds that pursued him. He told himself the war is over, this isn't real, you can't have me, and you can't come here. With tremendous effort he fought back the shadows. The detective broke out in a cold sweat. He thought, I've beat you before and I'll beat you again. I beat the malaria and I'll beat you too. Gradually the sound of the machine gun fire subsided, and the explosions grew quiet. The ground quit shaking and Chester could hear the rustle of the leaves in the wind. The breeze chilled him, because he was soaking wet with sweat. But, for now at least, it was over.

The police officer returned with another man wearing a suit.

"Mr. Brantley, this is Detective Sergeant Cayce."

Chester stood up and shook hands with the Sergeant.

He remarked, "Good to meet you Cayce."

Cayce replied, "Same here. You did quite a nice job on these guys tonight. It couldn't happen to a more deserving bunch of boys. So, these punks decided to try to kill you. Is that right?"

"Yeah, Danny said he had been given two grand to bump me off."

Cayce replied, "I don't guess he mentioned who paid him to do it, did he?"

"He claimed he didn't know the guy's name."

Cayce said, "Well that figures, these bums don't like to give up information. Are you working on a case?"

Chester replied, "Yeah, I'm checking out the death of a friend of mine in Orange. He and his wife, and his son all died within a few days of each other. When I started nosing around in their deaths, someone hired our boys to do a job."

Sergeant Cayce responded, "It's that simple?"

"Pretty much, it's hard to say until you get the guy you are after. You know what I mean."

"Yeah, I guess I do, Brantley. Who knows what a killer thinks."

Chester quizzed, "Have you done any investigating of the bombings?"

Cayce scowled, "The Army, and the FBI don't want any help. Word came down to stay out of it. Why? Does this involve the bombings?"

Chester responded, "Sam Lewis was killed in one of the first bombings in Orange under suspicious circumstances, his wife died of a suspicious looking suicide, his son was killed in a suspicious looking accident, the son's girlfriend was murdered, and his best friend was murdered, too. I've been looking into it, and there have been three attempts on my life. My gut level feeling is there is a connection, but I can't prove it as yet."

"I wish I could help you, Brantley. It sounds like you are standing pretty close to the solution."

"Chester lit a Lucky. "So, you weren't able to find out much about the bombings before they pulled the plug on you?"

"That's about the size of it. That's where you have it over us, Brantley. You can work on your own. The city fathers can't make you back off. I wish you luck."

"Maybe you can tell me something, Casey. Have you ever heard of a hood named, Blackie?"

Casey said, "Yeah, I've heard of him. No one seems to be able to hang anything on him. He supposedly is involved in prostitution, gambling, and different rackets. Why? Do you think he had anything to do with this attempt on your life?"

"Well, it was a thought. I had a tip that Danny was connected to Blackie, but he denied Blackie being involved."

Casey responded, "Blackie is a bad boy alright. We suspect he is one of the big guys. The truth is we know he is into the rackets, we just can't prove it. He lets cheap crooks like Danny do the dirty work. Is there anything else I can do to help?"

Chester replied, "Not that I know of, Casey. Do I need to sign a statement about what happened here?"

"Yeah, let's go inside the club. We've taken the place over and sent everyone home." Chester and Casey went upstairs to Danny's office. The door was unlocked.

Casey asked Chester, "Do you want a drink? The joint is full of alcohol and the employees took off after the shooting. I'm on duty but you're not."

"I could use Jack Daniels on the rocks."

"No problem, I'll get someone to get it for you. Here sit at the desk. Use this paper and just write out your statement in your own words."

Chester lit up a Lucky and Casey left the room. In a few minutes a rookie policeman brought Chester a bottle of Jack Daniels and a double rock glass filled with ice.

"Thank you very much," he said.

The officer smiled and left the room. Chester wrote out a pretty good description of the incident omitting his entry into Danny's office. He didn't mention the first attempt on his life either. By the time he had finished the statement and signed it Casey returned. Casey sat down and read the statement through.

"That should take care of it, Brantley. I don't expect any repercussions for you from this. I talked to the chief and he sounded pleased. Is there anyone over in Orange that would vouch for you if need be?"

"You could check me out with the medical examiner, or with Sergeant Logan of homicide. I think they would both vouch for me."

Casey said, "That will be fine. Okay you are free to go. Thanks for cooperating. Here's one of my cards. If I can help you out on a case sometime, let me know."

Chester replied, "Thanks a lot, here is one of my cards."

Chester said his goodbyes and walked to the Mercury. Luckily his car was spared bullet holes. He started up the Merc and drove back toward Orange. It felt good to be alive. All the leads keep coming back to the Army. Someone in the Army is behind the murders. It must be connected to a cover up. The detective knew he was running out of leads.

It was six in the morning when Chester arrived back in Orange. He drove to Rita's apartment. From the parking lot the detective noticed the lights were on in Rita's place. Rita never gets up this early and she couldn't be waiting for him, because he had called her. Chester decided to try to peek in the window. He quietly slipped up to the living room window. The blinds were nearly shut, but he could see in a little by the edge of the blind. He couldn't see anything at first. He didn't hear the radio playing and he knew Rita always played the radio when she was alone. Then he saw Rita dressed sitting in a chair looking intently across the room. Her lips moved, she was talking to someone. Chester began to sweat. He kept moving around trying to get a look at the person Rita was talking to. He couldn't see. He tried the other side of the blind, but couldn't see. The detective went back to the starting point. Rita was still talking occasionally.

Chester thought, what can I do? It must be a dangerous situation. If it wasn't; he wouldn't be embarrassed for being careful. He must assume there is someone in there with a gun. How could he get the drop on the guy without taking a chance on getting Rita hurt? The detective knew the people he was after wouldn't stop at murder. But, if they wanted to kill her, they could have done it already. Chester had been through these things before, but not with Rita in the middle. Oh, God. What was he to do? He had to do something, but what?

Chester sat down on the lawn. Suddenly, the ground began to shake, and he could here rifle fire. He saw people running. No . . . no . . . not now. The detective forced all his concentration to overcome the ghosts of the past. He told himself, pull out of it Rita needs you. Pull out of it, he thought. It isn't real, it isn't here, it isn't now. His head spun, he could see smoke and hear screams. Then abruptly the screams stopped, the ground quit shaking, and the smoke in his mind cleared.

Chester found himself sitting on the lawn covered with sweat and hands shaking. He quietly rose and walked a few yards away and sat back down. He lit a cigarette and waited for his hands to quit shaking. Other people can just fight in the present, but I have to fight in the past too, he thought. Why is life so difficult? By the time Chester had finished his cigarette the shaking had stopped.

The detective went back to Rita's window. Nothing had changed, but he still couldn't see. He tried every angle to see through the obscure blinds. Finally he caught a glimpse of a gun. Someone was sitting in the easy chair with a gun pointed at Rita. Now what should he do? He could shoot through the window, but what if there were two gunmen instead of one? He could kick in the front door and hope for the best. That was too risky for Rita. He could call the cops, but they would get her killed for sure. He could give himself over to the guy with the gun, but then they would both be killed.

Desperate times call for desperate measures. Chester walked to the alley. Very carefully he picked a trash can from the selection there. He found one with a lot of newspaper in it. He carried the can as quietly as possible into the building. All the lights were out except for Rita's. He carried the can down the hall to Rita's door. He stopped at the hallway phone. The detective called the operator and asked her to ring his number back in three minutes, claiming it wasn't working properly. He gave the girl Rita's number.

Chester lit the newspaper with his cigarette lighter. The paper began to smoke. The detective waived the smoke toward the door. The fire began to fill the can the smoke began to spread down the hallway. The fumes burned his eyes and nose. The smoke grew more intense. Suddenly the phone rang in Rita's apartment and Chester yelled, "Fire! Fire!"

The detective moved the trash can away from the door and waited he could hear a commotion coming from several of the apartments. People burst into the hall.

Chester yelled again, "Fire! Fire! Run for your life."

Rita's door opened and she came out coughing with a man holding her arm. Chester didn't hesitate. He jerked the man's hand away and delivered a smashing blow to the man's jaw. The man stumbled backward into the room. Another man threw himself onto Chester. The two of them toppled over just inside the door.

Chester yelled, "Run Rita."

He could have saved his breathe she was nowhere to be seen. The detective and his assailant rolled over locked in the struggle. Chester knocked the man's gun out of his hand and they wrestled across the floor. The detective noticed the other man was still struggling to get up. He drug his man to his feet just as the other man tried to enter the fray. Chester kept the man he was fighting between him and the other man. That way he only had to fight one man at a time. The other assailant was powerless to do anything with his comrade in the way.

Chester drove his fist deep into the stomach of the man, and struck him hard on the nose. The man went down in a spurt of blood. The second man jumped on top of the detective. Chester turned and threw the man over his shoulder onto the floor hard.

Two of the men living in the building found the burning trash can and used the hallway fire hose to extinguish the fire.

Chester turned to the man with the broken nose just in time to receive a bone rattling body block. Stunned the detective stumbled back against the wall. The man with broken nose ran out of the room and down the hall. The remaining foe struck the detective with a lamp and he fell to the floor. Chester did not see the man run out into the hall.

When Chester regained consciousness Rita was putting a cold cloth on his face.

"Where did they go, Rita?"

"Relax, Darling, they are gone. You have another knot on your head."

"Rita, did they hurt you?"

"No my white knight rescued me. Just lay there and relax for a few minutes."

Sirens wailed in the distance. The hall was full of people and smoke. The residents opened the hallway doors and got fans to clear out the smoke.

Firemen and policemen walked the halls trying to determine what happened. People were talking and wandering the hall and looking in at Chester on the floor.

Rita helped Chester on the couch and brought him an icepack for his head. She went into the hall to explain what had happened to the police. In time she returned and sat beside her man.

"You were wonderful, Chester. Those men were really scary and they said they were waiting for you. They have been here all night."

Chester said, "Oh my God. Were you scared to death?

"I guess I was, but I felt we would get out of it somehow. I didn't know you were going to burn the place down to save me."

"It wasn't all that bad. Just a little smoke"

"Well it worked, Sweetie. The bad guys took off when they thought we might burn."

A policeman knocked on the open door of the apartment.

Rita said, "Yes, can I help you."

The officer responded, "Yes, ma'am. I'm Officer Collins I need to get your statement."

Rita smiled and said, "Certainly officer come right in."

The officer got out his notepad and pencil, "Can you tell me what happened in your own words, ma'am?"

"Certainly, if you need my name it is Rita Richards. When I came home from work tonight, these two men were waiting for me. They pulled a gun and came into the apartment with me. They told me they would shoot me if I gave them any trouble. Then they sat up with me all night waiting for my boyfriend here to come over. I wasn't expecting him, but I was afraid to tell them that."

"Did they say what they wanted with your friend?"

"No they didn't. I tried to get them to talk, but they wouldn't tell me anything."

"What is your boyfriend's name?"

Chester spoke up, "I'm Chester Brantley. I'm a private detective; detective Logan in homicide will vouch for me."

Officer Collins remarked, "Yes, I know Detective Logan. Do you know the men that were here Mr. Brantley?"

"No, I don't think I have ever seen them before."

"Okay, Mr. Brantley, what is your side of the story?"

"I came over early about six o'clock. I noticed the lights were on and thought something must be amiss. Rita works nights and would normally be sound asleep by this time of the morning. I peeked in the window and saw a man holding a gun on her. I decided to create a diversion to avoid anyone getting hurt. So I set fire to a trash can and gave the alarm. The ploy worked and the two men came out with Rita. I separated the men from her and we got into a fight. They finally got the best of me and took off. I'm sorry about creating such a hullabaloo but these guys have killed before."

"Really, who have they killed?"

"I suspect they killed Romeo Pink the other night. In addition, Wanda Jennings was murdered possibly by the same bunch. Another fellow tried to kill me the other night at my apartment, but he died in the effort."

"Oh yes, I heard about that. Do you think this is connected to a case you are working on Mr. Brantley?"

"Yes, I do. Detective Logan is aware of the case I'm working on. You can ask him about it if you like."

"Can you give me a description of the men you fought with?"

"They were both wearing bright colored sport shirts and khaki pants. If and when we find them I think we will find they have military ID just like the man I was forced to kill in my apartment."

"How tall were they and what was their weight?"

Chester scratched his head. "I was pretty well occupied fighting with them. They were both about five-foot-eight, I would say. One was blond and one was black headed. They would weigh in at about one hundred and forty pounds. One of them has a broken nose and a lot of blood on his clothes. Oh, there should be a gun on the floor here somewhere that one of them had."

The officer got up and looked around. He moved some of the furniture and finally found a .45 automatic.

"Is this it, Mr. Brantley?"

"I would think so. That looks like Army issue hardware too."

"I see what you mean, Mr. Brantley. It looks like someone in the Army has it in for you."

Chester replied, "Yeah, it looks like I have been getting too close to the truth, doesn't it?"

"Do you have anything else to add Miss Richards?"

"No, I think that pretty well takes care of it. You don't think Chester will get in trouble about the fire and smoke, do you?"

"No, ma'am, I think drastic measures were called for. I don't think anything will be said about it. I'm just glad you two didn't get hurt. Mr. Brantley, you might want to take measures to protect Miss Richards until you get your case resolved."

Chester replied, "I whole heartedly agree. I wouldn't want anything like this to occur again."

The officer got up, "I will get out of your way and let you folks get some rest. This has been a harrowing experience."

The officer shook Chester's hand and Rita walked him to the door. The commotion in the hall seemed to be calming down. Most of the people were getting ready for work, but Chester and Rita were exhausted.

Rita asked, "Are you hungry, Lover?"

"I'd rather sleep."

Rita replied, "Me too. Let's go to bed, Handsome."

It was eight o'clock when Chester and Rita crawled between the sheets. The bed felt so good. The detective was so tired he fell asleep as soon as his head hit the pillow. He dreamed of guns, mobsters, models in jail, and cute little cab drivers. He chased gunmen all around Rita's living room.

CHAPTER SIXTEEN

Chester awakened to the phone ringing. Half asleep he stumbled around looking for the phone. Finally he found the receiver and answered, "Hello."

Rita's voice said, "Chester Brantley, who do you think you are? You promised me you wouldn't get into anymore gunfights, and then crawl in bed with me without saying a word. The paper says you killed three men this time. How many men will you take on next time, a half dozen? What are you going to do take on a whole mob by yourself? Well what do you have to say for yourself? You can kill three gunmen, but you can't even talk to one little woman."

Chester rubbed his eyes in an effort to get them open. He couldn't get his mind to work. "Well . . ." he said.

"Is that all you can say?"

"Well . . ."

"Chester, when you find your tongue, you had better come to Mack's." Then the phone went dead.

The detective sat down on the side of the bed. He looked around the room confused. His eyes still didn't want to stay open, and he couldn't make up his mind whether to get up or go back to sleep. He didn't even realize he still had the receiver to his ear. He decided to go back to sleep. Chester put the phone back on the cradle, and went back to his dreams. Things would look better later.

As evening approached, the detective awakened from his slumber. He could tell the light was waning. Chester was surprised that he had slept all day. He struggled out of bed in search of a cigarette and a glass of water. The recovering detective lit a lucky and drank a whole glass of water. He started coffee and sat at the breakfast table. He felt only half conscious.

When the coffee pot had finished perking, he poured himself a cup. The coffee tasted good. Maybe it would clear some of the brambles from his mind. Gradually the numbness began to wear off.

"Uh-oh, Rita." Chester checked his watch. The time was eight in the evening. He had slept for twelve hours. The detective showered, and shaved. He picked up flowers and drove to Mack's place. Chester came in the front door and sat down on his usual bar stool. Rita had her back to the bar at the time he came in, and didn't see Chester until she turned around. There he sat with two dozen carnations, and a beautiful box of candy. Rita's heart melted.

"Chester, how can you be so sweet, and at the same time so stubborn?"

The detective seemed at a loss for words. "Uh . . . with lots of practice?"

Rita laughed, "Oh, I give up. I can't stay mad at you."

Chester ordered a sandwich, and coffee. His eyes were still mildly swollen, and the numbness hadn't completely left him yet. He thought, wow what a night. The detective finished his meal and lit up a Lucky. He surveyed the bar. Half of the customers were soldiers. They were young guys mostly. They drank, laughed, and lived their lives like there was no tomorrow. Perhaps that was a good attitude for a soldier. Live life for the moment, for tomorrow you may die. Chester smiled, nothing like a brush with death to make a guy introspective.

The detective used the phone booth near the back door to check his answering service. There were no calls of importance. Chester thought of Joy.

He had the operator place the call for him, "Hello."

"Joy, is that you? This is Chester Brantley."

"Chester, I was upset when I saw the paper. Are you sure you are all right?"

"I'm fine. Don't let it upset you. Those guys tried to kill me and they got what they deserved."

"Don't worry; I haven't lost any sleep over them. Thanks for calling."

"I felt like I owed you that much Joy. You were helpful to me, and you are a very special girl."

"I want you to call me again, Chester."

"I will. Take care of yourself."

"I will, if you will."

Chester laughed, "That is a promise. Goodnight"

"Goodnight, Chester."

Chester returned to the bar. Jack wouldn't be in tonight, he thought.

Rita asked Chester, "Hey, Sailor, ready for the usual?"

The detective replied, "Let me stick with coffee for awhile, Angel."

Chester made an effort to relax. It was good to be alive. The detective knew he must take more action soon, but for now it was good to forego even thinking about it. Tomorrow would arrive soon enough.

"Chester?"

The detective looked around to see Detective Logan standing beside him.

"Logan, how are you doing?"

"I'm fine, Chester. I'm glad to see you in one piece."

"So far, so good."

"That's great, Chester. A detective called from Los Angeles today. I told him you are a good man."

"Thanks, Logan, I appreciate it."

Logan smiled, "The cops over there think you are aces. They've been trying to get the goods on those guys for a long time. You saved them the trouble. They said even the district attorney is pleased. That must be a first."

Chester smiled, "I appreciate the cooperation."

"How are things going on the investigation?"

"Logan, everything seems to lead back to the Army, or at least someone in the Army. Did you hear about what happened this morning here in Orange?"

"The police sergeant replied, "No, I didn't. What happened?"

"My girlfriend Rita was kidnapped and I had a big fight with the two guys in her apartment. I'm pretty sure they were soldiers, but I can't prove it. They got away."

"That is a shame. I would like to have a talk with those babies. As we discussed, my hands are tied when it comes to the Army. If I can help unofficially let me know."

"I understand, Logan. Thanks. I would like to ask one favor. I believe this case will domino pretty soon, but I'm worried about Rita after what happened last night. Can I buy you a drink?"

"No, thanks I'm on duty. I can arrange a police guard for three or four days on the strength of the kidnapping. Would that help any?"

"Sure three or four days would help me out a lot, Logan. I'd sure appreciate it."

Logan took out a pad, "What's her name?"

"Rita Richards, she works right here as a bar maid."

Logan thought a second, "Okay I'll have a man here in plain clothes within the hour. He will hang out in here when she is working and follow her home when she leaves. I'll use three men with eight hour shifts. How does that sound?"

"It sounds great, Logan, I have to be free to run down leads if I'm ever going to get to the bottom of what is going on."

Logan smiled, "I know exactly what you mean. Oh, yeah, I've got a package for you in the car."

"Really?" Chester followed Logan out to the car.

"Logan pulled Chester's shotgun out of the back seat. The grand jury cleared you on the shooting at your place. I thought you might need this back."

Chester smiled, "Thanks a lot, Logan. I hope I don't need it."

"Well, let's hope not. But, if you do; you've got it."

Chester and Logan bid each other fair well; and the private eye put his shotgun in the Mercury. He returned to the bar, and ordered a Jack Daniels. After an uneventful evening, Rita and Chester returned to her apartment.

When they were comfortable on the couch Rita said, "It is good to have you here with me, Chester. I get scared when I read the papers sometimes, but I know you can take care of yourself."

Chester replied, "I think things will come to a head soon. I can't stop trying to resolve all this. Just hang in there, kid. It should get better soon. I've arranged for a policeman to keep an eye on you for a few days. He'll be wearing street clothes. In fact he was there tonight. Did you notice him?"

"No, I didn't. Which one was he?"

"I'll point him out tomorrow. Rita, I have trouble saying it, but I love you. I was crazy with worry when I found you in trouble this morning. You are precious to me, Beautiful. No one could ever take your place."

Rita said, "Wow. I should get into trouble more often, if it is going to bring out your feelings this way. Chester, I love you. I adore you. I think I have loved you since the moment I met you. Every beat of my heart calls out for you."

Chester said, "You were very brave last night and this morning. I was surprised, anyone else would have fallen apart."

Rita smiled, "I have to learn to take things in stride if I'm going to be with you. I can handle it, Sweetheart."

The detective smiled, "You amaze me. You are the perfect companion"

"It's about time you figured that out, sailor."

Rita smiled and kissed Chester. They held each other close. Rita had a scintillating scent. Chester kissed her and felt all his desire rush through his body. She was everything. They got up and went to the bedroom.

CHAPTER SEVENTEEN

Thursday morning dawned on Orange, California resplendent with colors of yellow, and white reflected on orange sand and verdant green vegetation. Residents of the city awakened from their slumber to meet the challenges of the day.

Chester rose early to meet the dawn. He started the coffee and lit the first Lucky of the day. Sleeping all day yesterday and last night too, he felt good. The time to make his move was at hand. He was running out of leads to pursue. Everything seemed to lead to the troop trucks at Santa Anita. Chester and Jack had agreed to meet tonight.

The detective showered and shaved. He cooked a breakfast of bacon and eggs. He felt like a human being again. Chester slipped out quietly to avoid waking Rita. He noticed the police officer sitting in the black Ford in the parking lot. He drove the Mercury to his office. Joe was just opening the barber shop.

"How are you doing this morning, Joe?"

"I'm well, Chester, how about yourself? The paper said you had a little altercation with some boys in Los Angeles."

"Did you hear about two guys kidnapping Rita?"

"I take it she is okay?"

"Yeah, it took a hell of a fight, but I ran those guys off. They looked like off duty soldiers to me too."

"Chester, you really had an eventful day."

"The detective grinned, "Just routine, Joe. No, I'm just kidding. It was a little hairy there for awhile."

"Did you find out anything, Chester?"

"Danny Martin said an officer in the Army hired him to kill me."

"Like you said, Chester, it keeps coming back to the Army."

The detective sighed, "Yeah, it does, Joe."

"What's next, Ches?"

"Time to do some more snooping, Joe."

"Be careful, Chester, I wouldn't want anything to happen to you."

Chester smiled, "I feel the same way, Joe."

Joe smiled at the joke. "Let me know if I can help, Ches."

"I will my friend."

Chester took the elevator to the second floor and walked directly to his office. With his hand on one of his colts he opened the door. The office looked as it should. The detective placed his pistols on the desk, took off his coat, and sat down. He called the answering service to discover there were no important calls.

The detective lit up a Lucky and put his feet up on the desk. His heart told him to do one thing, and his mind told him not to. Decisions, decisions. He thought about the pros and the cons. He compared outcomes. He thought about the techniques he used in the South Pacific. He thought about diversions.

Finally, Chester got up and went to his car. As he approached the Mercury he noticed the hood was popped up slightly. He checked and the hood wasn't latched. He raised the hood and carefully looked over the motor. Near the starter something was amiss. *That doesn't belong there.*

On closer inspection, he discovered something wired to the starter. It was plastique explosive. Chester's hands began to shake uncontrollably. His knees felt like jelly. His head was swimming. He walked to the door of the car and sat down in the seat. He lit a Lucky with trembling fingers. He fought back the visions of the war. He kept telling himself to maintain, maintain. Gradually his breathing returned to normal and his hands quit shaking. He thought of Rita's face to help him relax. He told himself he would get through this and life would be good.

When he was satisfied that he was steady again, Chester went back to the front of the car. Carefully he eased the blasting cap out of the plastique and pulled the wire off the starter. Then he cut the tape holding the explosive to the starter and carefully brought it out. The detective placed the object of concern in the trunk of his car and wrapped it in a towel he had there. *Maybe I will give this back to them.* Chester thought better of it and drove to Lloyd's gun shop.

"Lloyd, Are you busy?"

"No, Chester, what can I do for you?"

"Look what I found." Chester unwrapped the cloth to display the Composition B.

"Where did you get that, Chester?"

179

"Somebody left it under my hood."

"Can you get rid of it for me, Lloyd?"

"Uh . . . yeah sure. I'll set it off out in the desert when I'm out there shooting."

"Okay, Lloyd, here is the blasting cap. You know how to use this stuff, don't you?"

"Yeah, no sweat. Take care of yourself, Chester."

"I will."

Chester thought, whew, what a day. Chester drove around to make sure he wasn't being followed, and stopped off at the hardware store. He bought bolt cutters, flares, two flash lights, a penlight, a spool of wire, and two pair of handcuffs. After loading everything into the trunk he drove to Rita's place. She had already gone to work. Her note said she would see him later. He made himself a double and lay back on the couch. He spent the afternoon resting and planning.

He drank sparingly to keep his head clear.

Seven o'clock that night found him in Mack's Bar waiting for Jack. Rita was hurrying around taking care of customers. Jack was nowhere to be seen, but the evening was young. Chester nursed a drink to make it last. After three attempts on his life, the detective felt he must go forward. Eventually they would get him, if he didn't get them first. Those trucks are so near, but so far away. He thought, maybe I'm getting obsessed. Chester checked his watch, it was eight. Jack may have decided not to risk it. Rita grinned at him when she passed. Chester smiled and tried to look light hearted. Customers came and went, the bar was jumping tonight. Soldiers gathered in the pool room talking and laughing, but still no Jack. Time crawled.

Chester went over his plan in his mind. He made changes and went over the details again. He checked off the list of things to take. Then he went over the whole plan once more. The detective checked the clock again. He thought, where in the hell is he? I can't do this by myself. Maybe I can. Let's see, how would I do it? Chester rubbed the back of his head vigorously. He took out his fountain pen and made a drawing on a paper napkin. He lit another Lucky and ordered another drink.

Rita smiled and teased, "What's up, sailor? Shore leave tonight?"

Chester looked up and smiled, "Cinderella liberty, due back at the ship by midnight."

"It's hard to get one up on you, Lover. I get off at midnight. Do we have a date?"

"I had an appointment with Jack, but it looks like he is standing me up."

"Okay, if he doesn't show, I'll be your backup date."

"Now, you're talking," he said.

Ten o'clock came. To be followed by eleven. Three forevers later mid-night came. Rita, put on her jacket and came to Chester's side.

"I guess you are stuck with me, Sailor."

Chester smiled impishly, "I'll just have to make the best of it."

The two lovers walked together to the Mercury. He put Rita in the passenger seat and took a flashlight out of the glove box.

"I want to check the water. It won't take a moment, Rita."

Rita smiled, "You don't want to hold up a hot date."

"God knows that's true." Chester replied.

The detective raised the hood carefully, and checked everything carefully. Satisfied that all was well, he lowered the hood. Chester drove around long enough to ensure safety and then drove to Rita's.

Chester decided to just relax for the rest of the evening. Rita made them a sandwich and they had a night cap. These times alone are so nice, he thought. I hope they never end. Rita didn't notice that the detective put his .45s on the chair beside the bed. While she took off her makeup, Chester slipped one of the revolvers under his pillow. After Rita fell asleep, he took a section of wet newspaper and folded it. Then the detective forced it under the door to make a door stop. Finally he tilted a chair and put it under the front door knob. He thought, that is about all I can do without tipping Rita how dangerous things are getting. Chester lit one last cigarette and smoked it sitting in Rita's easy chair.

Chapter Eighteen

Morning found the detective asleep in the easy chair. The irrepressible sun awakened the sleeping prince. He rubbed his eyes. The sandman had visited last night. Chester's eyes were swollen. He got up and went to the sink. Washing his face helped. He started breakfast. The detective had the feeling that time was suspended. Here in this room, alone with Rita, somehow everything was on hold. Outside the world was barreling toward a climax, at least for him it was. But, not here, here everything was sweet and loving and disconnected from killing and death. He knew that the next few days would make a big difference for him and Rita. Things would either get better, or they would get a hell of a lot worse. Chester had experienced this sensation of timelessness before big battles in the South Pacific. Although this heightened feeling of awareness was no stranger, it still made him feel odd.

The detective ate his meal and lit a cigarette. It was good to rest before the battle. Nothing to do, but take your ease while you can. He looked out the window and felt the warmth of the sun and saw people going about their business. For others it was business as usual.

Chester spent the morning resting and waiting for Rita to wake up. When she got up they ate together and he gave her a ride to work. Then he drove to a men's wear store and bought two black shirts, pants, watch caps, and jackets. He went by Lloyd's gun store.

"Hey, Lloyd, what's up?"

"Not much, Chester, what can I do for you?"

"I have a strange request. Do you have a 22 with a silencer?"

"I have one with a very thick barrel that just makes a snap. Would that work?"

"Probably, can I hear it?"

"Sure, let's go downstairs to the shooting range."

In the basement of his store Lloyd had a firing range set up. Lloyd brought the 22 he was thinking of down stairs with him. He loaded it and let Chester fire it. It made a snap like a cap gun.

"Is that too loud, Chester?"

"It would sound pretty loud at night, Lloyd."

"Okay, let me show you something."

Lloyd reached into a box of parts. "This is a muffler for a lawnmower. I just attach it to the barrel of the 22. Now, try it."

Chester fired the pistol again. It made a quick muffled spewing sound.

"That is much better. I'll take it like just like that, but I don't understand what makes it work."

"A silencer is just a larger chamber added onto the barrel of the gun, to give the escaping gases a bigger area to expand into before entering the air. That is what muffles the sound. I'll wrap it up for you, Chester."

"I need two switch blade knives, too."

"No problem, Chester. That's what I like a two gun, two knife man."

"Not exactly but close, Lloyd."

Chester drove to Mack's Bar and ordered the usual from Rita. He sat back and waited to hear from Jack. Late that afternoon Jack walked in.

"Hi, Chester, I'm sorry about last night. I missed the bus again. I made good use of the time though."

Chester asked, "So you are still in?"

"I wouldn't miss it for the world."

"Now, you're talking, Jack. Hang on let's use the back room."

Chester got Mack to let him use the back room. The two comrades in arms moved to the privacy of the back room. A table and chairs were set up there adjacent to stacks of cases of beer.

When they were comfortable, Chester asked, "Okay, what did you find out, Jack?

"I spent most of the night on the roof of Santa Anita watching those guards. I watched them walk their posts until four in the morning. They came on duty at ten and were relieved at three. I know that is a long watch, but I'm beginning to think that is their only duty. Anyway, they walked their post smartly until midnight and then they started taking long smoke breaks. They meet where their posts come together and as time goes on they get more and more lax. They know everyone is asleep. They talk and laugh and just goof off. Now, from this center point, they don't have a good view of the anything but the front of the trucks actually. Now, I figure if we could knock out the light at the far end of the enclosure it would be dark at that end, but well lighted where they will be. What do you think, Chester?"

The detective smiled, "You did an excellent job of reconnoitering, Jack. I'm impressed. Are you sure you haven't seen any action?"

"Not yet, I haven't."

"Well, you are catching up fast.

Chester explained about the clothes and equipment he had picked up for them. He outlined a place to park the car, how to cut the fence, and how to repair it afterwards to avoid detection. He laid out the escape plain and rules of engagement. They should avoid harming the guards, because they may be innocent soldiers. Stealth was the keyword of the discussion. They would remain silent as they had before when they were in the area. Each would have certain tasks to do. They would make their move at 01:00 hours (1 a.m.). Chester brought the equipment in the back door. The two men rehearsed what to do, and how to use the equipment.

After going over everything several times Chester said, "Are you up for this tonight?"

"I'm ready, if you are."

"Okay, let's eat a light diner, one or two drinks to relax, and we leave at o dark thirty (12:30 a.m.)."

Chester put the equipment back in the car. He checked under the hood one more time, and clamped a gum wrapper under the hood. The detective went inside for a sandwich. Rita cruised by and took his order. Jack sat with him at the bar. It felt good to have a plan of action. With a little luck there would be no more bombs under the hood, no more apartment ambushes, and no more bodies littering the landscape. At the very least, he was taking action. He wasn't just waiting anymore.

When Rita came by Chester said, "Hey, Gorgeous, a friend of mine said he used to date you, and that you are a great kisser. Is that true?"

Rita smiled and said, "The man is a liar. No man could stand to lose these lips."

Chester laughed, "Did I ever tell you I love you?"

"Just once."

"Consider yourself told."

Rita put her hand on Chester's and gave him the warmest look he had ever seen.

"Rita, you are the wind through the willows, you are a baby's first smile, you are everything to me."

"Chester, what's up with you tonight? That is beautiful."

"Oh, I don't know. I've just been thinking about how much you mean to me. You should know how I feel, even if it's hard for me to say."

"Yes, you are right, Chester."

"Do you have another Jack Daniel's left?"

Rita replied, "Just one left in the bottle, sailor. Coming right up."

Chester rubbed his cheek, as he watched Rita go about her work. He averted his eyes to avoid tears. He thought, I'm getting soft. When Rita brought his drink, he downed it and turned to Jack.

"Are you ready, soldier?"

"Lead the way."

The two warriors walked out to the Mercury. Chester checked to make sure the gum wrapper was still there, which it was. He drove to a road that entered the woods near the barracks. The detective parked the car. The cohorts changed into the black clothes. Chester gave one of the switchblades to Jack along with the bolt cutters. The detective took the 22 with the silencer, and the spool of wire. Silently they crept through the woods.

When they reached the clearing, Chester positioned himself where he could see the guards. He watched as they approached each other in a half hearted march. They stopped and lit up cigarettes. He waited for the two men to get involved in conversation. Then he took careful aim at the flood light located on his side of the trucks. He squeezed off a shot directly at the bulb. There was a quiet "sput" and the light went out. The guards didn't seem to notice.

When he was satisfied, he led Jack in a crouch across the darkened lot. The two friends crouched beside the fence using the bolt cutters to cut the wire. Silently they peeled back the fencing to allow entry. Chester held the fence for Jack and then Jack returned the favor. Chester left the spool of wire by the makeshift entrance.

The two men crawled to the closest truck. Jack watched the guards from under the truck while Chester silently slit the canvas on the side of the truck with his switch blade knife. Very carefully and slowly he climbed into the truck. He shielded his pencil light to avoid detection. The truck was loaded with small cardboard boxes. The boxes were extremely heavy. He thought, what could weigh this much. The detective opened his switchblade and cut one of the boxes open. Carefully he shined his light into the small box. There in the gloom was a golden reflection. It was a gold bar. What did this mean? Chester's pulse began to race. How could this be? This can't be, but it was. Stealthily he looked around to assure himself all these boxes looked the same. They must all contain a gold bar. The boxes are just for concealment.

Chester used his knife on the soft metal to carve off a piece the size of a silver dollar. He needed proof. This should open some eyes. Without a sound the detective closed the box and placed it under some others to conceal it. Carefully, very carefully, he slipped out of the truck and back to the ground. He looked at the guards still talking, and pointed toward the fence. The shadowy figures made their way to the fence and crept through the hole. They used the spool of wire to repair the fence. No one would notice, now. Chester and Jack retraced their steps across the vacant lot, and through the woods to the car.

Chester started the car quietly, and idled out of the woods, before accelerating on down the road.

When they were clear of the camp Jack said, "I can't stand it any longer, Chester, what did you find?"

The detective grinned at him and placed the piece of gold in his hand.

"What is this?" Jack held the fragment of gold up to the window as they passed a street light. "My God, it's gold."

Jack sat staring at the object in his hand with his mouth open.

"What does it mean?"

"It boggles the mind, but it must mean that the general relieved the Germans of tons of gold. Reggie discovered the gold, and the general has been bumping off people to cover it up ever since."

"Chester, we did it. We solved the case."

"First, we have to convince the authorities. That may be difficult, but that little piece of gold should help. We have to act fast though, before they move the trucks. If they manage that, we'll have a hell of a time."

"I see what you mean. What do we do next?"

"It can wait till morning. Then I'll get a couple of my friends in on it. I don't think it will take too long to clear up this mess. At least, I hope not."

"Can we celebrate tonight?"

"Yes, I would say a celebration is in order. You did a good job tonight, Jack. That took real nerve."

"Whew, I'm just glad it's over."

Chester understood how Jack felt. He felt free for the first time in days. He felt vindicated. With the window half down the night air smelled good. Life will be a lot better after this mess is straightened out. The detective could feel it.

Chester pulled the Mercury into the parking lot of Mack's Bar. He couldn't wait to see Rita. The back door of the bar was open. He could hear people laughing and see them milling around. The two smiling friends walked side by side across the lot.

Then two men with guns stepped in their way in the dimly lit parking lot. Two more men appeared behind them.

Chester grabbed for his .45s, but the man in front of him snapped back the hammer of his gun.

"Mr. Brantley, don't think I won't shoot you here. I just don't give a damn. Others will be hurt."

Chester stood motionless for a moment before deciding to wait.

"Who are you?" the detective asked.

"Let's just say you killed an associate of mine the other night. Relieve, the gentlemen of their guns. Don't worry, Mr. Brantley, you won't be needing weapons. We are going for a little ride."

Jack said, "So you followed us?"

The man with the gun replied, "Followed, what followed, we have been waiting here for you all night."

Chester spoke up, "Of course you didn't follow us. I don't know what you are driving, but I doubt it could keep up with my car."

"Okay, hot rod, let's go."

Chester gazed longingly at the back door of the bar. To be so close to safety . . . .

The armed men accompanied Chester and Jack to a limousine. They put the two friends in handcuffs and placed them in the back of the limo.

Chester reflected, "Pretty nice car for a crook."

"We borrowed the general's staff car in your honor."

"That was very thoughtful of you," said the detective.

The limousine drove out to Santa Anita and through the front gate. It pulled into a fenced area, and the men got out of the car.

Chester asked, "What's this?"

"Mr. Brantley, you are to be the special guest of our stockade for awhile. I trust you will enjoy the accommodations."

The detective smiled, "Charmed, I'm sure."

Chester and Jack entered the stockade and were escorted to a cell. In the adjoining cell a tall man lay on a cot asleep. The two newcomers decided to try to get some rest. Chester's watch said three o'clock. They reclined on the two cots in the cell. Finally, they dozed off.

Chapter Nineteen

The morning dawned in sunny California. Orange residents greeted another Friday. Reports of bombings and other acts of violence were down the last couple of days. Perhaps things were getting better after all.

Rita couldn't sleep. Chester hadn't picked her up last night. She found his car in the lot on the way home. What did it mean? Where was that man? Who could she call? What could she do?

The medical examiner went about his business not knowing that Chester was missing. Charley, the editor of the newspaper, was starting his day unaware that the detective needed help.

The prisoners at the Santa Anita barracks slept through the early morning hours. The exertions of the previous day and night had taken a toll on them. There is little to do when incarcerated anyway. The guards let their charges slumber. It meant less work for them.

The stockade consisted of a small office for the guards, and two small cells in the adjoining room. The guards had a desk, a heater for winter, a filing cabinet, three chairs, and a clock on the wall. The cells were furnished with two cots, a toilet, and a very small sink each. In addition, each cell boasted a twelve inch square window with bars. Bars provided three walls of the cells with a wooden back wall.

The guards played poker to distract themselves. Slowly the morning ticked away. At eleven the turnkey roused the prisoners. He brought them coffee and sandwiches. Chester and Jack sat up. They drank the black coffee and ate the sandwiches. The two friends noticed the prisoner in the next cell still lay on his side with his back to them.

Chester called out, "Hey, soldier, you need to take what you can get. Chow is on. Hey, buddy, are you okay?"

The tall soldier slowly rolled over to face them.

"Colonel Stewart, what are you doing here?"

"I could ask you the same thing, Chester."

"My God, this is crazy."

"Chester, you are a lot closer to the truth than you think. Here let's pull our cots over to the bars that join our cells. We can talk while we eat. Keep your voices low."

"Colonel, how long have you been here?"

"They snatched me a few days ago. Chester, who is your friend?"

"Colonel, this is Corporal Jack Turner. He helped me discover the secret those trucks are concealing."

"Nice to meet you, son. What is the secret?"

"Then, you don't know about the gold?"

"What gold, Chester?"

"I don't think our little play mates are aware of it, but we got a look in those trucks. The ones the general has under guard.

They are loaded with gold bars. There must be thousands of pounds of the stuff."

"Well now, greed seems to be the motive for this craziness. I'm not sure why they grabbed me, Chester. They haven't told me anything. Maybe, it's because I was checking on Reggie Lewis. Could that have anything to do with it?"

"Yes, Colonel, I think that would be very likely."

Chester ate his food thoughtfully. He rubbed the beard stubble on his cheek. The detective tried to put all the pieces of the puzzle together.

Finally Chester remarked, "Colonel, my guess is that the general stole three truck loads of gold from the defunct German government. He had it loaded by the colored guys in his outfit. After which, he has been killing them, and anyone they may have talked to."

The colonel quizzed, "You mean to keep anyone from knowing about the gold?"

"Yeah, I figure that must be what is in back of the whole thing."

The three men finished eating in silence. After lunch, Chester said, "I can't figure why they didn't kill me last night. They have tried to kill me three times. Why would they want to keep me alive, now?"

"They're saving us for something, Chester. But, for how long is the question."

"The men that nabbed us last night were armed and prepared to kill. What about the guards?"

"They are the general's men. They are hard cases, Chester. If you look out your window, you can see there are armed guards outside. The general doesn't want anyone discovering we are in here."

"I'm afraid that doesn't bode well for us, Colonel."

"Someone should be looking for me by now."

Chester explained, "The general is telling everyone you went to Germany on a special mission for him."

"Damn," the colonel retorted. "What about you, Chester? Does anyone know you are here?"

"There are a couple of people that have a pretty good idea what I have been up to. They have been told to call in the cavalry if something happens to me. But, I don't know how long it will take for someone to realize something has happened. Have they tried to grill you or anything, Colonel?"

"No, they brought me in here at gun point, and it has been total boredom ever since."

"Apparently, all we can do is watch for an opportunity to take the guards. Baring that, we are at the general's mercy. Speaking of which, you haven't heard anything from him?"

"No."

The colonel looked dejected. He sat with his hands folded. Nothing seemed to make sense for him. For the first time in his life, he was waiting for something but he didn't know what. He had no control over his life or the lives of others. He reclined on the cot and rolled over to face the wall.

Chester watched the colonel for a period of time. He motioned for Jack to come close.

"Jack, the colonel isn't handling this well. I don't think we will be able to depend on him for much help."

"Yeah, he seems to be taking it hard."

"You've been pretty quiet yourself, Jack."

"Are you okay?"

"I'm not accustomed to being around colonels."

"I understand," Chester said. "This is the plan, watch for an opening. Grab a guard or a gun if the opportunity presents itself."

Jack said, "I'll keep an eye out."

"Remember, Jack, these guys are killers and a fortune is at stake. There is nothing they wouldn't do."

Jack nodded comprehension. The two friends lay down to rest while they waited for their chance.

The afternoon ticked by slowly. The guards looked in on the prisoners a couple of times. The prisoners, for lack of anything else to do, slept.

Back in Orange, Rita was frantic. She had not heard from Chester. She didn't know who to call or what to do. She called the police, but was told it was too soon to report him missing. She went to work in hopes that the detective would walk in. Chester's car still sat in the lot. She talked to Mack about her concerns. He appeared to be as much at a loss as she was. She left work and walked to Chester's office. There was no sign of him there. She went back to work.

At six in the evening the guards roused the prisoners. They brought them food once again. They were to feast on a sumptuous meal of rice and beans with black coffee. One guard brought the food into the cells while the other guard watched with his hand on his military .45.

Chester called out to the colonel, "Colonel Stewart, you need to keep up your strength."

The three men ate in silence. The camp was quiet outside. The prisoners settled down for the night.

David Bruce

At ten that night, the door burst open. The prisoners awoke with a start. Before them stood the general in full dress uniform. He was accompanied by the four men who had taken Chester and Jack.

"Stand at attention for the general."

Chester replied, "I don't think so. If the general doesn't like it, he can come in here and make us."

The man who had done the talking the previous evening was dressed in a major's uniform. Another man wore a lieutenant's uniform. The other two men wore MP uniforms.

The Major offered, "Shall we discipline them, sir?"

"No, let them sit on their bunks if they wish."

The general said, "Mr. Brantley, you have given us quite a bit of trouble. You are very accomplished at staying alive. I checked your service record. You were good at staying alive in the South Pacific theatre, also."

Chester replied, "It seemed like the right thing to do at the time."

"Quite so. You earned the Purple Heart, also. I could use a man like you, if you were so disposed."

"I have a job, General. Thanks just the same."

"Yes, you are a man of value."

The general stood five foot six, one hundred and forty pounds, he paced back and forth like a bandy rooster. He was dressed like MacArthur in kakis with gold braid on his hat, with the addition of twin nickel plated .45 automatics. This guy had real issues.

"General, I would love to hear the whole story. I have figured out a lot of what is going on. But, it would help me a great deal to hear your side of this campaign."

The General said, "You mean you might be persuaded to join us?"

"Well, sir, as an investigator my services are for hire. However, I always need to learn the particulars before I can make a decision concerning taking a case. Of course, it isn't a question of morals. A detective must represent either side of an issue. It is very much like an attorney client relationship. Everyone has the right to representation in court, and everyone has the right to the talents of an investigator. That is if the party in question has the money to pay for these services."

"I understand your position. Perhaps when you learn the goal of this campaign, and the progress we have made you will be persuaded. Major we'll take Mr. Brantley with us to my office."

The colonel seemed to be ignoring the conversation. Jack gave Chester a confused look.

"I'll be back later, Jack."

The general offered, "You can bring your associate with you, Mr. Brantley. We will eat, and drink, and discuss the campaign."

The general led the way, followed by Chester and Jack, with the general's men bringing up the rear. They all got into the limousine, and rode through the stockade gate and across the camp to headquarters. Again, the general lead the men to his office. He took off his hat and told the men to take a seat.

"Major, have steak and lobster brought from the officer's mess for our guests. Mr. Brantley, we have already eaten, however we will join you in drinks. Lieutenant Carnes, do the honors. Gentlemen, what will you have?"

Chester ordered a whiskey on the rocks, and Jack ordered a beer. Jack caught Chester's eye and raised his eyebrows quizzically. Chester smiled at him and returned the look.

The general said, "Before we begin, are there any questions you would like to ask, Mr. Brantley?"

"General Huff, I was just wondering, how much gold is there loaded on the trucks?"

The general smiled, "My, you are a resourceful man. To answer your question, there is a total of six thousand five hundred pounds. You can imagine, with gold valued at thirty seven dollars an ounce. We are talking about a total value in the neighborhood of three million eight hundred and forty eight thousand dollars American. Quite a tidy sum, wouldn't you say?"

Chester whistled, "Yes, sir, I would say so."

Chester noted a slightly maniacal look in the general's eyes. The officer offered his guests cigars from his hand carved humidor. Chester took one. Jack declined the offer.

The general leaned back in his chair and lit his cigar. Chester sniffed the fine tobacco before lighting up. He puffed and smiled his satisfaction.

The detective took note of the major. He was a tall man, about six foot four, stocky but not fat, with short red hair, and clean shaven. The officer wore an expensive watch, and tailor made uniforms. He had the smell of money on him, but it was impossible to tell if he came from money or had ambitions for wealth. The major appeared to be a mover of men, but not really a leader. He wasn't the kind of man you could depend on in a pinch. He was the kind that could send you over without a thought. He could have you fed to the dogs over brandy and cigars.

Lieutenant Carnes was a much more passive man. He stood five foot five inches tall, one hundred fifty pounds. He was well suited for the service, because he was willing to take orders and carry them out without question.

The general reveled in Chester's appreciation of the cigars. "Now, gentlemen, let me begin at the beginning. While pursuing the Nazis, I discovered that high ranking officers of the Third Reich had cashed away a huge stock of pure gold bars. Seizing the moment, I captured the gold, and had the remaining German officers shot. The next step was to load the gold into unobtrusive troop trucks and transport my new found wealth to a ship."

The orderly brought Chester and Jack their food. He set up a table for them close to the general's desk so they could talk easily.

Chester interrupted, "That would be the USS Terrell."

The general raised his drink, "Exactly, salute, Mr. Brantley. You are a very remarkable man. Of course, it took a little time to make arrangements to bring the gold home. Once we arrived in the states we were forced to remove certain security risks. You may have guessed that we created a diversion to distract the populace from what we were doing. Because of my rank and connections in Washington it was a simple matter to commandeer this duty station, as a stopping off point for the gold."

"Just for clarification, General, can I safely say that you used colored men in your outfit to load the trucks, and effectively eliminated them afterwards for security purposes?"

The general laughed, "You should have been an officer, Mr. Brantley. Yes, you could safely assume the foregoing."

Chester took a deep drink from his glass and said, "I take it the Terrell was scuttled in order to cover up as well?"

"It wouldn't do to leave any loose ends."

Chester looked to Major Haynes and Lieutenant Carnes occasionally to see how they were taking this discussion. The major appeared to be suspicious of the detective, however the lieutenant seemed to be immune to any such negative thoughts.

Chester quizzed, "What would be our next step, General?"

"Preparations are being made to transport the gold to a Swiss account. My small group of associates will then be paid. This will complete phase one of my grand plan. Phase two will involve using a portion of the money to get myself elected president of the United States. You see, Mr. Brantley, our beloved country is ripe for the taking, by a general. It is time for the military to take the helm. Our voters will be justly grateful for the winning of the war."

"Well, sir, can I prevail upon you to tell me what part I play in the grand scheme of things?"

"Of course, Mr. Brantley, you will be indispensible as the leader of my security forces once I take office. It is obvious that you are a very careful man. I'm sure you will be just as careful for your president."

Chester replied, "You will make an exceptional commander in chief, General."

The general said, "I take it you have decided to cast your lot with us. Am I right, Mr. Brantley?"

"Well, General, I hate to seem crass, but we haven't mentioned remuneration as yet."

"Right you are. How does a hundred thousand a year sound?"

"That sounds like a nice round figure, sir. You are a very persuasive man. May I ask how many of us are in on the deal."

The general replied, "Just a handful of officers and men."

"Well then, it is settled, General. When do I start?"

"Major Haynes will remain in touch with you. You can consider yourself on retainer. Of course, you will refrain from investigating this unpleasantness any further."

The detective responded, "Of course, sir. I dislike being petty, but I would like my revolvers back."

"Major Haynes will take care of that for you. Now, gentlemen, I will retire for the evening. It has been a most fruitful meeting of the minds. I bid you goodnight."

The men stood at attention and gave the general a smart salute. He returned the salute and marched out of the room. Chester turned to face the Major.

Chester said in a conspiratorial tone, "Can we speak privately, Major?"

"Yes, you men can wait outside."

Jack and the lieutenant left the room with the two MPs.

"Would you like another drink, Mr. Brantley?"

"You can call me, Chester."

The major went to the bar and prepared two drinks. The two men sat down facing each other.

Chester said, "There is no two ways about it. The general is off his rocker. He couldn't possibly have gotten the gold this far on his own. You must be the real brains of this outfit."

The major smiled, "The general is right about you being a very discerning man. Yes, you are right, General Huff is certifiable, but he has the rank and the connections to pull this off. All we have to do is wait for him to get the gold converted to cash. Then we can take our share and go our separate ways. He'll probably end up in a funny farm, and nobody will believe his ravings anyway. I'm glad you said what you did about the General, Chester. If you hadn't I would have known you were stringing him along. That would have caused more unpleasantness."

"I understand, one must be careful, but what will be my cut. He'll never make it to the White House."

"Let's say a one time payment of a hundred thousand. Is that enough to buy your efforts and your silence?"

"Let's shake on it." Chester stuck out his hand, and the major clasped it. The detective was surprised at how limp the major's handshake was.

The detective asked, "Can you have someone give us a ride back to town?"

"I'll have one of the guards take you."

"I'd like my .45s back, too."

"Yeah, they're at the stockade. I'll have the guard get them for you. I'll call you when I need you."

Chester and the major walked out of the office, and on outside followed by the other men. The major instructed one of the guards to take them home and pickup Chester's revolvers.

Suddenly the sound of small arms fire reached them, followed by a loud explosion. Then all hell broke loose. Two cars came barreling through the camp spraying machine gun bullets. The men hit the ground. Chester could see that the MP beside him was dead. He rolled him over and took his .45 automatic out of the holster. He pushed back the slide and took off the safety. He began firing at the second car as it came by. Bullets hit all around the men on the ground. Chester was able to hit the car several times. The two vehicles sped on by.

"Jack, are you okay?"

"I think so, Chester, but look."

The detective looked around to see the major, the lieutenant, and the other MP were all dead.

"Damn, here, grab this one's .45. What the hell is going on?"

The two friends could hear yelling, and gunfire, along with more explosions.

"Come on, Jack, we had better get to the stockade."

Chester and Jack ran across the camp. They had to get to the colonel. They ran as fast as they could. No one challenged them. The lead spitting cars had cleared the way for them. When they arrived at the stockade, they found the door open and the guards gone. Quickly Chester searched the desk and found the keys. He sent Jack to release the colonel, and finding his guns, he put them back in the slings under his arms where they belonged. He felt better already. In the top drawer he found a set of jeep keys.

Jack returned with a sleepy eyed colonel. Chester helped pull the officer toward the outside door.

"Here jump in this jeep. This is the right key, I hope. Here, Jack take this .45, that will give us two each."

The vehicle started and Chester slammed it into reverse and burned rubber away from the area. The two cars came careening back through the camp followed by the three troop trucks. The two cars were still firing at anything that moved and throwing out explosives. The stockade burst into flames as the convoy passed by.

Chester pulled in behind them. As they neared the front gate they could see the barrier was down and no one occupied the guard house. The troop trucks shot through the exit and, out onto the highway bouncing and swaying. Chester pursued them as closely as he dared.

"Colonel, Stewart, you are breathing free air again." He looked at the older man.

"Are you with me, Sir?" The colonel didn't reply.

Jack said, "Who are these guys? They can't be the cops."

Chester replied, "No, they're just as bad as the general's men."

Then they saw on the side of the road a large car on fire.

As they passed it Chester said, "That was the General's limo. They got him, too."

The detective eased back on the throttle to let the trucks have more of a lead. He decided to turn the lights out for a time to make the truck drivers think they weren't being followed. The night was dark, but he could see to follow by the tail lights of the trucks.

As they drove along Jack remarked, "For awhile I thought you were going over to the other side, Chester."

"I would have said anything to save our hides, Jack. I still don't know if that major believed me or not. I don't guess it matters, now. It's nice to be alive, isn't it?"

Jack laughed, "I was never so glad to be alive."

Chester said, "Snap out of it, Colonel. Things are looking up. You have a lot more battles to fight."

As they went under a street light the older man smiled at Chester. The detective breathed a sigh of relief. The old man would come out of it in time.

The detective turned his head lights back on, and kept a steady pace to avoid losing the trucks ahead. The road was abandoned this time of night. People still didn't drive much at night with gas rationing being fresh in their minds. The road stretched out ahead endlessly. The trucks led on through the darkness of night. The chase went on for an hour and a half.

Jack asked, "How are we doing on gas, Chester?"

"We are doing fine according to the gas gage. Let's hope it works right. Wow. What a night, huh?"

"You can say that again, Chester. Do you suppose we will make it out of this in one piece?"

"We will, if we don't do something stupid. Jack, do you have any idea where we are?"

"I saw a sign that said Riverside, Chester."

"Jack, these guys have to stop sometime. It will be light soon and these army trucks stick out like a sore thumb."

The Colonel offered, "They would need to switch trucks."

Jack and Chester jerked their heads around in surprise. The colonel was smiling at them. They both smiled at the officer.

Chester said, "Glad to have you back, Colonel." They all laughed.

The landscape began to change. Grass and trees began to change gradually to houses and buildings. Then it happened,

Chester realized he couldn't see the trucks anymore. He sped up, but that didn't help.

"Jack, where did they go?"

"I don't know, Chester, they were there a minute ago."

Chester turned around and drove back slowly. He looked up and down the side streets. He watched the buildings as they passed.

"Help me watch as I drive around. They could have turned off or pulled in a building. There are a number of warehouses and shops around here."

The detective drove up and down, looking. He tried a couple of turns, but found nothing. He circled around a few blocks, but still nothing. Finally, he pulled up and parked. He lit a cigarette and offered the pack to his companions.

"I lost them like a green kid. The sun is coming up, now. They must have turned off their lights, and pulled in a building or turned off somewhere. I feel sure those trucks are in this neighborhood somewhere. What do you guys think?"

The colonel remarked, "The Army often gets trucks off the road during the day to avoid detection. When it gets dark again, they start to roll again."

"I'm guessing you are right, Colonel. Let's go eat, I think I saw a café back a little way."

Chester started the jeep and retraced his steps till he found the diner. The three friends got out and went in. They had steak and eggs, with lots of coffee. When they finished breakfast, they had another smoke and tried to relax.

Suddenly Jack sat bolt upright. "Oh, my God, I just realized I'm AWOL."

Chester and the colonel looked at each other and starting laughing.

Jack retorted, "It's not funny, I've never been late back to my duty station."

The colonel smiled, "Don't worry son, you can't be absent without leave while you are with me."

Jack looked relieved, "I didn't think of that."

Chester said, "That's okay, Jack, that just shows you are conscientious. Colonel, I wouldn't be surprised if Jack got another stripe over this. What do you think?"

The colonel grinned, "At least one, I would say."

Chester said, "If you don't mind, gentlemen, I'll lead the discussion." When no one spoke up, he continued. "I for one would like to continue the chase. I just won't have closure until I recover the gold, or at least find out who took it. However, I can handle things from here if you two want to return. What do you think?"

Jack said, "I will do whatever you want me to do. I would be glad to go with you."

Chester offered, "How does this sound? Colonel, I could send you back with Jack. He could bring back my car and we could try to take up the chase again tonight. In the mean time you could inform the authorities, but we need to keep things quiet. If the papers carry the story of the gold, the trucks will really disappear. If an army of cops or soldiers descends on this area, the trucks will again disappear. So, I suggest they give me one more night to try to smoke out the gold."

"I think I can hold them off for a short period of time, Chester? While we are going back, where will you be?"

"We can find me a hotel room. That way I can make a few calls and rest."

The colonel replied, "Then it is settled. Let's ask the waitress about a room for you."

Chester paid the bill and asked about a room. The waitress suggested a small motel down the road a short distance. The detective checked in, and bid the other two men farewell. He gave Jack the keys to the Mercury. He went into his bungalow and lay across the bed. It felt good. He put in a call to Rita.

"Hello."

"Rita, honey, are you okay?"

"Oh, Chester, I've been worried sick. Are you okay?"

"I am fine."

"What happened, Darling? I thought something awful happened to you."

"Jack and I were captured right in Mack's parking lot."

"Where are you now?"

"I'm in Riverside, but I should be back to town sometime tomorrow."

"How did you escape from the men that took you?"

"Angel, it's a long story. I'll tell you everything when I get back. But, be happy, Sweetheart, this whole mess will be over soon. Try to get some rest, everything is going to be all right."

Rita forced back the tears, "I can't wait to see you, Chester. Take care of yourself."

Chester hung up the phone and breathed a sigh. He called Charley at the paper, and briefly outlined the events of the previous evening. He asked the editor to keep the information about the trucks out of the paper for the time being.

He repeated the same procedure with the medical examiner.

The detective turned the radio on and fell asleep. For the first time in days he could really relax. He snored as he often did when he was really exhausted. He didn't hear the sweet sounds of Count Bassie and his orchestra.

Chester awakened to a knock on the door. He looked out to see Jack standing on the little porch. It was one in the afternoon.

"Come on in, Jack. Let's get some rest."

The room had two beds. Chester didn't have to tell him twice. Jack crawled into the other bed and was sound asleep within minutes. Chester went back to his bed and slipped into a deep slumber.

CHAPTER TWENTY

When Chester awakened it was early evening. It was not completely dark out yet. He showered quickly and dressed. Jack was beginning to rouse.

"Jack, you had better get a move on. We will want to eat, and it's getting dark."

"Yeah, you're right."

Within in a few minutes the two men were in the car on the way to the diner. Chester said, "I don't think they will move the trucks till later. However, we can watch the road from the diner."

Chester and Jack made a meal of meat, and potatoes with coffee. They lit up and relaxed a few minutes with another cup of coffee.

"What do we do, Chester, just sit on the side of the road and wait for the trucks?"

"That is probably as good a plan as any, Jack. If it doesn't work we can take a look at some of these warehouses around here. We can even hang around here a while, but we have to be ready to move."

Jack asked, "Did you call Rita?"

"Yeah, she was frantic. She'll be okay, though."

"Did you call Flo?"

"No, I'll call when this is over. She won't be worried."

Chester laughed, "You don't think she'll be worried when she hears about the barracks being destroyed?"

"Gee, I didn't think about that. Maybe I should give her a call."

"Use the pay phone over there. I'll watch the road."

In a few minutes, Jack returned smiling. "Chester, you were right. She was really excited."

"Is she okay, now?"

"She will be all right. Women are such a pain."

"They could say the same thing about us. What do say to taking a six pack with us, Jack?"

"I'm with you, Chester."

The detective drove the Mercury to the approximate spot he lost the trucks. He pulled off the road and drove up on a grassy knoll. He got out of the car and opened a beer with the church key the waitress gave him at the café. Jack opened his beer and sat down on a stump. The evening air was refreshing.

Jack asked, "Chester, have you figured out who these guys are yet?"

"Well, it can't be the good guys. It must be someone who found out about the gold. Someone with access to machine guns. You don't suppose it's the mob, do you? That might explain the explosives they were using, too. I really can't think of anyone else crazy enough to take on the Army."

"Well, if we are after the mob, we need to be very careful."

"Right you are, Jack. It's not too late to go back. This business could still be very dangerous."

"I didn't mean to imply that, Chester. In fact the Colonel gave me a letter assigning me to you for a few days."

"He did? Well that's good. Now, we can prove you aren't AWOL. I'm glad you stayed in these black clothes instead changing to a uniform."

"I don't even know if I have any uniforms besides the one in the trunk of the car. They may have burned up at the base."

"Damn, I didn't think about that, Jack. When this is over, I think they will dissolve the barracks anyway. The Colonel will need to get the quartermaster to give you new uniforms if necessary. Let's get another beer."

The two friends opened another beer and talked at length about the war, the events of the last two weeks, and their thoughts about the future. They finished the six pack and half of a pack of Lucky Strikes. The road was abandoned for the most part. Two cars passed but no trucks.

"Here comes a truck, Chester."

"It's about the right size, too." They were poised for action, but the truck turned out to be a white bakery truck. "False alarm, Jack."

It was close to midnight. The night air was getting nippy. Chester zipped up his jacket.

Chester remarked, "If they are going to move those trucks, it's getting to be time to do it. Let's make another run to the dinner, to see if it's open."

Chester and Jack hopped in the car and drove back to the diner. Luckily it was still open. Chester bought sandwiches, a thermos of coffee, two packs of cigarettes, and even another six pack. They brought their provisions back to the little knoll and resumed their vigil. They ate the sandwiches with a beer, saving the coffee for the wee hours of the morning. After a couple of hours another truck approached. Again they rose in anticipation only to realize it was another Whittier Bakery Truck.

Jack remarked, "This is like the army, hurry up and wait."

"You have that right. Stake outs are tough."

Chester and Jack began to pace back and forth to warm up. The road was clear. The wind was chilling.

The detective suggested, "We could get back in the car, Jack, to warm up?"

"It is getting uncomfortable out here. Let's have some of that coffee."

They waited in the Mercury. The two friends kept talking to avoid getting sleepy.

Finally Chester said, "Let's drive up by those warehouses. Maybe we will see a light on or something."

They drove down a couple of the side streets, but everything seemed quiet. Chester drove back to the main road. Just as he approached the highway he saw a warehouse door go.

They watched as a white truck pulled out and started down the highway. Chester gave the truck a lead before turning in behind it.

"Chester, what are you doing? It's just another one of those Whittier Bakery trucks."

"I've got a hunch, Jack. I think that is one of the troop trucks with a white paint job and some metal side plates attached for camouflage. That would explain why we are seeing another truck every two hours. That way no one gets suspicious."

"Chester, if you are right, that's great. What tipped you off?"

"Well, I cheated, Jack. I noticed one of the tires on that last truck had a big spot of white paint on the right rear tire. That happens sometimes when you are in a hurry with a paint job. The tires looked like the type of mud tires the Army uses, too. What would a bakery want with mud tires?"

"Okay, I'm sold. What do we do, now?"

Chester answered, "We just follow them, without losing them this time."

The Mercury followed the truck on through the night. Once in a while Chester would turn the headlights off, in order to lessen the chance of discovery. During one of those periods of driving without lights, a car came charging out onto the road behind them. It was driving without lights, also. The car accelerated hard in an attempt to catch the Mercury. Chester heard the approaching auto before he saw it.

"What the hell is that?" he said.

Something told Chester this was no cop. He slammed the pedal to the floor, and the Mercury exploded down the road. Chester turned on the lights to avoid hitting anything. The vehicle behind them followed suit. The Mercury was gaining distance, when the car behind opened fire. Bullets pierced the night like speeding fireflies. The reports sounded like pistol fire. The Mercury was flying down the highway. It overtook the bakery truck in short order. The car with the shooters was way behind, now. Chester passed the truck, and sped down the road. When he felt he was sufficiently far ahead, he slowed way down and pulled up in a farmer's driveway and extinguished his lights.

The truck passed the driveway with the car as an escort. Chester waited for a full minute before backing out of the farmer's road without lights. He could make out both sets of tail lights.

Jack said, "Now what?"

"The only thing I know to do is follow way back and make sure we are following two sets of tail lights. If the car's lights disappear we should stop, because they will be waiting for us again. Maybe they are getting close to where they are going. Where are we? Have you seen a sign?"

Before long they saw a sign but had to stop to read it. They couldn't read it without the headlights. When Jack shined a flashlight on it, the sign said Paradise Lodge Lake Arrowhead three miles. Chester kept up the distant tail.

"This is tricky, Jack. We can't afford to lose them, and we don't want a gunfight either."

The lead vehicles were only doing fifty miles per hour, so they weren't that hard to follow. Lake Arrowhead looked uninhabited at this hour. Chester finally turned his lights on, but kept his distance. He could barely make out the tail lights ahead. Finally, he saw them make a turn. Slowly the detective proceeded.

"Let's just drive casually. I'm betting they didn't get a good enough look at the car to recognize it."

As they idled by, Jack said, "I saw them up that last side street, Chester. It looked like they were stopped."

"Okay, let's park the car and walk up there."

Chester and Jack parked the car and walked up the side street, staying in the shadows. As they approached they could see the truck, and the car sitting in the street. A garage door opened and both the truck and the car drove in and down a ramp. The garage door closed behind them. Chester got a good look at the garage, and got his bearings by the adjoining houses. Silently he motioned for Jack to follow him. They walked back to the Mercury, and got in.

Chester said, "Let's see if we can find a diner open. There should be one around here somewhere. This is a big fishing area, and fishermen get up early."

Two streets down they found a diner, and went in. They ordered breakfast and coffee. It had been a long night.

"Jack, we have to watch our step. This town used to be mobbed up during prohibition. They had bathtub gin, prostitution, speakeasies, gambling, and the whole nine yards. You could buy one drink or a carload back then. Apparently, the mob still has holdings here. Did you notice the truck and the car went down a tunnel?"

"Yeah, I caught that. What is a house doing with a tunnel?"

"It must have been a speak ten years ago. That way they could pull the beer trucks in."

"Chester, what do we do now?"

"We need to get a couple of fishing rods and some tackle. That way we can blend in with the locals. I think that house backs up to the lake. Maybe we can rent a boat and watch it from the water. I have the binoculars in the trunk."

"Chester, don't we need to call somebody?"

"Right, we'll call in the marines. Then we will just wait for them to come help us finish the job. Let's wait an hour or two. It's only six in the morning. I don't suppose the colonel gave you his phone number, did he?"

"Yes, I forgot, he was afraid you might not have it with you."

Chester smiled, "He was right."

Chester and Jack relaxed for an hour and then found a phone booth near the dock. Chester called the colonel.

When the officer answered, Chester said, "Good morning, Colonel."

"Chester, are you okay?"

"Yes, Sir, we had a hair raising night, but we made it. We have followed the trucks to Lake Arrowhead. We know where they are holding them, but we need more men to take them. Can you mobilize help?"

"Yes, Chester, Military Intelligence and the Treasury Department are in on it."

"Colonel, I think they need to come with a limited number of men, and dressed as fishermen. If we tip our hand the crooks might make a run for it."

"Chester, do you know who took the gold."

"Colonel, it could only be the mob. They had all kinds of rackets going here in the thirties. I'm guessing they still have a presence here. We don't want a bunch of uniforms and marked cars coming up here to this little village. They will stick out like a sore thumb."

"Yes, I see what you mean. Can you call me back in a half hour, Chester? We can arrange a time and place for you to meet with these men."

"Yes, Colonel, that will be fine."

Chester and Jack bought fishing tackle and rented a boat for the day. The detective called Rita to assure her all was well. He called Charley to let him know the story was reaching a climax. With luck it could be in the morning paper the next day. Chester called the Colonel back.

"Colonel Stewart?"

"Yes, Chester, is there a place you can meet these men about six this evening?"

"I will meet them at Sam's Diner by the dock at six. Will that work, Colonel?"

"Yes, that will be fine. Take care of yourself, Chester."

"Yes, Sir, I will."

CHAPTER TWENTY ONE

"Okay, Jack, let's catch a few fish. We can get some beer and take it with us. There's nothing more natural than two fishermen drinking beer. Have you still got the .45s we commandeered?"

"Yeah, I have them under my jacket, Chester."

"Good hold on to them. You might need them before this is over."

They bought a small ice chest, and filled it with beer and ice. They dropped anchor right across from the house they were watching. They baited their hooks, and started fishing.

"If you want to, Jack, you can lie down in the bow of the boat and take a nap. You can use the life jackets for a pillow."

"I don't think I could sleep anyway, Chester?"

The two friends whiled away the day. They caught a few fish, drank a few beers, smoked a lot of cigarettes, and told a lot of jokes. Chester noticed he was getting a little sunburned. The house had been quiet all day. From their vantage point they could observe the street in front of the house, too.

At half past five they came back to the dock. They dropped off the fishing gear at the car, and went to Sam's Diner. They took a booth and ordered steaks. When they finished their meal, they drank coffee while they waited. At six two fishermen entered the diner and walked directly to their booth.

One of the men asked Chester, "Have you guys been here long, Chester?"

"We arrived early this morning. Have a seat." Chester lowered his voice. "Are you guys carrying ID?"

The two men flashed their badges. "I'm agent Simms, Treasury Department and this is agent Thackeray, Military Intelligence. We didn't have any trouble recognizing you gentlemen. Colonel Stewart gave us a good description."

Chester smiled, "I was wondering how you were so sure of yourself."

"You have the location of the trucks established?"

Chester drew a map on a napkin. "This is where the house is located. When the truck went inside it went down a ramp. So the appearance of the place is deceiving."

Simms said, "You have done a good job, Mr. Brantley. You uncovered the whole thing and ran it to ground. I assume you would like to see it through to the end. Am I right?"

"Yeah, I would."

"Okay, then let's get down to brass tacks. I have ten men here. They're dispersed in the village. Some are fishing on the dock, a couple are in a lodge, a couple more in a restaurant, but we will all come together to enter the house at midnight. That way, civilians won't get in the way. I can get you men a room so that you can rest for awhile. I understand you had a long night and day."

"That sounds good, doesn't it, Jack?"

"It sure does. We could get a shower and a shave."

Chester smiled, "Maybe the Treasury Department would spring for a change of clothes at the tackle store, too."

Simms smiled, "I think the expense account can handle that for you. Are you ready to go, now?"

Chester and Jack stood up and lead the way to the tackle store. They picked out shirts, khaki pants, tee shirts, socks, fishing hats, and razors with shaving cream. Simms got them a room at the Paradise Lodge.

"Get some rest, gentlemen, I will meet you back at the diner at eleven thirty. It is open all night, I checked."

Chester called the desk to leave a call for eleven. He and Jack showered and shaved, and collapsed into their respective beds. At eleven the phone jarred them into wakefulness.

Jack said, "We just got here."

Chester offered, "Maybe we can catch up when this is over. I'm about ready for it, too."

Chester and Jack dressed and walked down to the diner. They ordered coffee. Within a few minutes Sims joined them.

"Did you get some rest?"

Chester replied, "Some."

"The house has been quiet. We have observed a little movement in the house, but that is about it. We are ready to move in at midnight. We can go in through the garage. We will pick up one more man on the way. Thackeray will enter by the front with four men. Four more men will enter from the back. That will leave one man in the street, as a sort of command post. We are all wearing black arm bands to avoid accidentally shooting each other. Here are yours. Any questions?"

Chester looked to Jack and then back to Simms, "That should do it."

Chester and Jack put on the armbands and followed Simms. They walked toward the house. On the way they met a fourth man, who joined them. The street was dark as they approached the house. Simms and the other man used a crowbar to pry the lock off the garage door. They opened it quietly.

The men used flashlights to light the way down the ramp. At the bottom of the ramp they could see the trucks backed up to a loading dock. They could hear the sound of a commotion up inside the house. They heard the sound of men running and gun shots. Agent Simms and his companion ran up the steps of the loading dock with Jack close on their heels.

Chester hesitated. He thought he heard something ahead. He hurried forward just as the sound of a powerful motor reached him. At the end of the tunnel an indoor dock came into view. A door was sliding open, offering access to the lake. At the dock a speed boat was revving up for a quick getaway.

Without hesitation Chester ran and jumped into the back of the boat, just as the powerful boat speed out into the lake. The driver looked around to see the detective flying toward him. The two men rose onto their feet locked in a struggle. They fell onto the deck of the boat, as the boat propelled forward at tremendous speed. Luckily there were no obstructions close by. The detective found his opponent to be very strong. They rolled back and forth. Chester struck his assailant twice on the jaw, with little affect. The mobster discovered a wrench laying on the deck and struck the detective on the forehead. Chester was dazed. The mobster looked up to see a dock looming directly ahead. He braced himself to jump, but Chester tripped him and he fell back into the boat. The detective dove into the water just before the powerful vessel hit the dock, and burst into flames.

The water was cold, but refreshing. Chester swam to the shore and struggled out of the water. He walked up onto the dock toward an adjoining house. The owner of the house came running out.

"Oh, my God, what happened?"

"We had an accident. Do you have a water hose? Maybe we can put the fire out ourselves."

Chester and the homeowner extinguished the fire on the dock, and the speed boat sunk effectively putting its fire out. After waiting fifteen minutes, the detective could see a boat coming. As it neared the dock, he heard Jack's voice.

"Is that you, Chester?"

"Yeah, it's me."

"Are you hurt?"

"No, I'll live."

Jack asked, "Where did the speedboat go."

Chester replied, "Straight down."

The detective got in the boat and they rode back across the lake.

"I think we got all of them, Chester. Some of them put up a fight, though."

"Did any of the cops get hurt, Jack?"

"No, everyone made it through it. Simms recognized several of these guys. They are all gangsters."

Simms was waiting for them at the house when they got back. He smiled when he saw how wet Chester was.

"So, Chester, did you enjoy your swim?"

"Not particularly. Man it's cold."

"Why don't you two go back to the lodge and call it a night? I saw the speedboat blow up. Will we be able to find it?"

The detective grinned, "You go to the burned dock and then turn straight down."

"I understand. Sleep well. We can get your statements tomorrow."

Chester took a hot shower and crawled into a welcome bed. Then, he called the newspaper and asked for Charley. Luckily he was there. Chester gave him the story about the recovery of the gold, and the capture of the mob. Charley thanked him and got busy on the story. The American public would be relieved to find out the bombings were stopped. They could rest easy. The Third Reich would not be rising from its own ashes like a phoenix. Bridges would be spared from sudden nocturnal damage. The National Guard would not need to guard train stations anymore. Honest German Americans wouldn't need to face wholesale discrimination. Reggie's friend Eddie Conner could go home and resume his life. Chester could quit entering rooms with drawn guns. He wouldn't have to sleep with a revolver under his pillow, or check for bombs under the hood. He could go back to carrying one Colt .45 instead of two.

CHAPTER TWENTY TWO

Noon the next day found Chester and Jack slowly waking. The shades on their window had kept out the sun for them and allowed them to get some much needed sleep. Chester sat on the side of the bed and lit a Lucky. He felt as if he were rising from the dead.

The detective remarked, "This must be the way a mummy feels."

Jack was smiling at him from his bed. "Chester, it all seems like a dream now, huh?"

"Or another life." Chester offered. "A hard life, too."

Jack said, "If we ever wake up, let's go eat. I'm starved."

"Jack, will you go get my suit and your uniform out of the trunk of the Mercury? My clothes are still wet."

"Sure, Chester, that is a step back toward normal life."

The detective and the corporal showered, shaved, and dressed. They walked down to the diner to eat. Simms was sitting at a table.

"Here, join me, gentlemen, did you have a good rest?"

Chester smiled, "Yeah, we feel a lot better. Food sounds good."

Agent Simms motioned for the waitress. The men ordered coffee, steak, and eggs.

Simms spoke up, "Chester, the guy you took down last night was Blackie Parone. He was the brains of the outfit. He was a gangster out of Chicago during prohibition. I think we pretty well cleaned out the gang last night. A couple of his guys bought it."

Chester inquired, "Did they have any ties with the general?"

"No, not that we know of."

"Then how did they know about the gold?" quizzed the detective.

"We found out that Blackie's nephew was in the Fighting Forty-ninth. We figure the kid got wind of the gold and told his uncle. The temptation to take three million in gold was too much for Blackie."

Chester offered, "The two men who ran my friend off the road had connections to a gangster named Blackie. Maybe it was the same guy, if so it could be that these two guys got wind of the gold and told Blackie.

"That very well could be, Chester. We will probably never know for sure."

Jack asked, "Then the bombings, and killings should be over?"

Simms said, "I'm sure that part of our history is behind us. Thanks to you two gentlemen. By the way, I'm working on getting the Treasury Department to pay you guys a reward for the recovery of the gold. Maybe I should say for the discovery of the gold, since it was captured German gold."

Chester asked, "Do you think the German government will raise a stink wanting the gold returned?"

Simms smiled, "They can try. However, they would be smart to take the war reparations they will be getting, and keep quiet about it. But, we'll leave that to the politicians. By the way, Jack, Colonel Stewart told me to give his regards to Staff Sergeant Jack Turner."

Chester laughed, "What do think of that, Staff Sergeant?"

"That sounds good to me."

Simms smiled at the newly made non commissioned officer. "I'm sure that is one promotion that is well deserved."

Simms had Chester and Jack give their statements for the record. It took a couple of hours. Chester and Jack bid farewell to Simms. They checked out of the lodge, and loaded up for the return trip to Orange. It seemed like a short drive after the ordeal they had been through.

"Hey, Jack, we had better call the colonel to see where you are billeted, now. I don't know whether your bunk made it through the fire or not."

When they got back to Orange, Chester called the Colonel.

"How are you doing, Colonel?"

"I am well, Chester. How are you men doing?"

"We are doing fine, and back in Orange. Does Jack still have a billet at Santa Anita?"

"Yes, Chester, but he can take a couple of days off. Just have him ask for me, when he returns. Did he hear about his new rank?"

"Yes, sir, and he is very proud."

"Well, he deserves it. You two really saved the day."

"Okay, Colonel, thanks for everything."

"No. Thank you, Chester. You will never know how grateful I am to you."

"That means a lot to me, Sir. Have a good evening."

Chester checked Jack into a hotel, near the circle, and invited him to come with him to Mack's place. Then, he made a bee line to the bar. They parked in the back parking lot and started toward the door. They didn't notice two men enter Mack's ahead of them. When they opened the door, the place was dark. They stood there unable to see anything. Suddenly, the lights came on and a crowd of people yelled, "surprise." Everyone was startled to see Chester and Jack standing there with guns drawn. Silence filled the room for a few seconds.

Chester turned red, and put away his revolver, "Sorry, it's been a trying week."

Everyone laughed. Across the bar hung a banner that read, "Welcome Home Heroes." Everyone gathered around the surprised warriors, shaking their hands, and slapping them on the back.

Rita ran forward and hugged Chester. "Hey, sailor, got shore leave tonight?"

"Yes, ma'am. I sure do, but not Cinderella liberty this time."

Rita's eyes filled with tears, "I'm so glad to have you home, Sweetheart."

Jack smiled, "Not half as glad as I am to be here."

Chester, Jack, and Rita had a wonderful time. It seemed like the whole town had turned out to see the returning champions. The detective and the new sergeant found that their money was no good. The drinks were on the house.

Chester felt free for the first time since VE Day. Joe the barber was there, along with the regulars at Mack's place. Mack was serving beer with both hands and so happy he could burst.

Chester asked Rita, "Do you need company tonight?"

Rita replied, "I think I'm going to need company a lot now."

"I'm sure that can be arranged."

Joe came by to shake hands. "Chester, you did a great job."

"Thanks, Joe."

"I'll be by for a haircut tomorrow."

"Sure thing, Chester."

The party ended when the bar closed, and the tired detective went home with Rita. They cuddled in bed and reveled in being together again. Their hearts were filled with love and affection.

CHAPTER TWENTY THREE

The next morning Chester and Rita slept in. the city could make it through one morning without the detective's vigilance. The paper was full of praise, but the lovers didn't care. The answering service was swamped with new business calls, and those of well wishers. Joe bragged to his customers of Chester's exploits. Herb smiled as he read the story in the newspaper. It was nice to know he had been of help.

In the afternoon, Chester called Eddie Conner to tell him it was safe to go home. He picked up his mail at the post office and returned Wanda's letters to her mother. He assured her that Wanda had been avenged.

The detective went by his apartment to change clothes. It felt good to be home with no MPs coming through the door. He went to the office. Everything was back to normal. He went by the barber shop to get a haircut.

Joe had a big smile on his face when he saw him walk in.

"How is everything, Chester?"

"I am just trying to calm down, Joe."

"Your life has been pretty exciting the last three weeks, huh?"

"Too exciting, Joe. How about lowering my ears for me?"

"No problem, hop in the chair. Chester, the paper was kind of sketchy about this general. Can you clear that up for me a little?"

"Sure Joe, in fact as my employer you should get a typed report giving you all the details. I can do it for you tomorrow."

"You don't need to go to that much trouble, Chester. You already sent me one report before the general got into the act."

"It's no trouble, Joe. Let me tell you about the general. While fighting the war in Germany, he stumbled onto six thousand five hundred pounds of pure gold bars. He was probably nuts already, but the gold must have pushed him over the edge. He commandeered the gold, and killed the Nazi officers that were holding it. Then he used the USS Terrell to transport his ill gotten gains back here. The general then started this reign of terror to divert attention from the fact that he was having anyone who knew about the gold killed. That's why Reggie, Sam, Georgia, Wanda, and Charles Pink were killed. Reggie found out about the gold and the general was trying to keep it quiet."

Joe said, "So the motive was greed?"

Chester replied, "That and the lust for power. The general wanted to be president."

"Well, thank God we had you to stand up to these guys, Chester?"

"Joe, let's hope there will always be Americans to stand up to maniacal little men that want to sell us out for money or power."

Joe replied, "Well said, my friend."

When Joe finished his haircut, he handed Chester two one hundred dollar bills.

"What is this, Joe?"

"That is the pay for the other ten days on the case. Is that right?"

"Sure, that's right. Thanks Joe."

Chester paid for his haircut and drove to Rita's apartment. He picked her up and they went back to San Clemente for a two day vacation. On the way, Chester realized that he hadn't gotten the shakes during the attack on the barracks, or during the chase. That was a real improvement.

He said aloud, "Yes, sir. Things are looking up."